Presents

Enjoy eight new titles from Harlequin Presents in August!

Lucy Monroe brings you her next story in the fabulous ROYAL BRIDES series, and look out for Carole Mortimer's second seductive Sicilian in her trilogy THE SICILIANS. Don't miss Miranda Lee's ruthless millionaire, Sarah Morgan's gorgeous Greek tycoon, Trish Morey's Italian boss and Jennie Lucas's forced bride! Plus, be sure to read Kate Hardy's story of passion leading to pregnancy in *One Night, One Baby,* and the fantastic *Taken by the Maverick Millionaire* by Anna Cleary!

We'd love to hear what you think about Presents. E-mail us at Presents@hmb.co.uk or join in the discussions at www.iheartpresents.com and www.sensationalromance.blogspot.com, where you'll also find more information about books and authors!

Royal Brides

Billionaire businessman Sebastian Hawk and
Sheikh Amir bin Faruq al Zorha are bound by
one woman: Princess Lina bin Fahd al Marwan.
Sebastian has been hired to protect Lina—
but all he wants to do is make her his. Sheikh
Amir has arranged to marry her—but it's his
virgin secretary he wants in his bed!

Two men driven by desire—
who will they make their brides?

Last month…

Forbidden: The Billionaire's Virgin Princess

Sebastian Hawk is strong, passionate
and will do anything to claim the woman
he wants. But Lina is forbidden to him and
promised to another man….

This month…

Hired: The Sheikh's Secretary Mistress

Sheikh Amir has a convenient wife lined up
by his family. His requirements: no love,
but plenty of heat in the bedroom! But he's
becoming quite inconveniently attracted to
his sensible secretary. Now Amir wants to
promote her—into his bed!

Lucy Monroe

HIRED: THE SHEIKH'S SECRETARY MISTRESS

Royal Brides

HARLEQUIN®

TORONTO • NEW YORK • LONDON
AMSTERDAM • PARIS • SYDNEY • HAMBURG
STOCKHOLM • ATHENS • TOKYO • MILAN • MADRID
PRAGUE • WARSAW • BUDAPEST • AUCKLAND

ISBN-13: 978-0-373-23511-7
ISBN-10: 0-373-23511-9

HIRED: THE SHEIKH'S SECRETARY MISTRESS

First North American Publication 2008.

This edition published by arrangement with Harlequin Books S.A.

® and TM are trademarks of the publisher. Trademarks indicated with ® are registered in the.United States Patent and Trademark Office, the Canadian Trade Marks Office and in other countries.

www.eHarlequin.com

Printed in U.S.A.

All about the author...
Lucy Monroe

Award-winning and bestselling author
LUCY MONROE sold her first book in September
of 2002 to Harlequin Presents. That book
represented a dream that had been burning in her
heart for years: the dream of sharing her stories with
readers who love romance as much as she does.
Since then she has sold more than thirty books to
three publishers and hit national bestseller lists
in the U.S. and England. But since selling that first
book, the reader letters she receives have touched
her most deeply. Her most important goal with
every book is to touch a reader's heart, and it is this
connection that makes those nights spent writing
into the wee hours worth it.

Lucy started reading Harlequin Presents books
very young and discovered a heroic type of man
between the covers of those books—an honorable
man, capable of faithfulness and sacrifice for the
people he loves. Now married to what she terms
her "alpha male at the end of a book," Lucy believes
there is a lot more reality to the fantasy stories she
writes than most people give credit for. She believes
happy endings are really marvelous beginnings, and
that's why she writes them. She hopes her books
help readers believe a little, too…just like romance
did for her so many years ago.

Lucy enjoys hearing from readers and responds
to every e-mail. You can reach her by e-mailing
lucymonroe@lucymonroe.com.

For my homegirls on my blog
(http://lucymonroeblog.blogspot.com/)—
I love our discussions, your enthusiasm
for romance and my books, and just having the
chance to chat with you every day. Thank you
for taking the time to be a part of my life.
You all rock!

PROLOGUE

"PLEASE, YOUR HIGHNESS, let me alert the sheikh to your presence." Agitation laced Grace's usual even tones as the doors to Amir's inner sanctum opened.

But then his family tended to have that effect on people—though rarely his always efficient and coolly composed personal assistant. Five years of exposure had almost made her immune, but an unexpected visit from a family member they'd both thought in Zorha was enough to unnerve even her.

Amir stood up behind his sleek, glass-topped desk. "I see you are still harrowing the help," he said to the tall man who'd opened not one, but both of the double doors leading into Amir's office.

Grace made an offended sound at his use of the word *help* while his brother simply strode into Amir's office with a somber air that belied the possibility of a simple family visit.

"To what do I owe the honor of your arrival?" Amir asked.

He had a feeling he already knew the answer, but admitting knowledge was as good as admitting culpability and he was not willing to do that…yet. But he should never have gotten involved with Tisa. The sex kitten had a love affair with the paparazzi that few could rival. However, at the time, Amir had needed a diversion badly and he had seen Tisa as the answer. For a while it had even worked.

Zahir did not answer, but simply stared at Amir for several tense, silent seconds. Being the youngest of three brothers had taught Amir many things, one of which was when it was politic not to talk. Now happened to be one of those times. He would not make the mistake of breaking the silence first.

He traded oblique look for oblique look with the man that could have been his twin but for the seven years that separated their ages.

They shared the same dark hair worn neither too short nor too long. While Zahir's was styled in a way that reeked businessman, Amir wore his in an artful tousle. They also shared the same square jawline, angular cheekbones and aquiline nose. All three brothers were tall, but he topped their brother Khalil by an inch, and at six and a half feet tall, Zahir exceeded them both in height. Taking after their father, they all had whipcord-lean bodies. Amir's muscles bulged slightly more from his time in the gym while Zahir showed the development of a man who spent time several hours a week riding. They were both dressed expensively, but while Amir favored designers like Hugo Boss, his eldest brother wore cool Armani.

Their matching brown-eyed stares did not waver until Grace cleared her throat and their attention swung to Amir's willowy assistant.

Below her red hair that was pulled back into a severe bun, her perfectly formed nose was wrinkled with displeasure. Full pink lips adorned with nothing but clear balm tilted in a downward curve. Behind the narrow dark frames of her glasses, her hazel eyes shimmered with disapproval at the brothers' stare down.

"Is this a meeting you need me for?" she asked Amir pointedly.

Bless her. Unquestionably loyal, she was

letting his brother know that while Zahir might be in line to their father's throne, it was Amir who called the shots here in his New York office. She was also subtly encouraging his brother to answer Amir's initial inquiry without him having to repeat it.

Zahir might ignore him, but he would not show bad manners by dismissing Grace's question with his silence.

Zahir stepped forward and dropped a tabloid on the desk. It was quickly followed by one after another, each folded open to the page of interest—if the story wasn't on the cover, which it was with most of them. Every headline screamed some lewd innuendo about *The Playboy Prince* and his latest conquest.

Amir grimaced.

Grace made another noise of disapproval. And Amir had no way of knowing whether that disapproval was directed at him or his brother for bringing the scandal sheets into his office. Grace didn't think much of the revolving door in his bedroom, and she'd let him know it on more than one occasion.

Zahir looked at Grace. "You have something you wish to say, Miss Brown?"

Grace might be shy in most circumstances

outside her role as his personal assistant, but here, she was in her element. No doubt, he was her employer. However, there was also no question that she reigned supreme in his office. At least in her own mind. They'd had a few *discussions* about that fact as well over the years.

She gave them both a look of displeasure. "I don't know which one of you gets the wooden spoon for having the poorest taste—Amir for getting involved with a media hound or you for bringing that trash here into the office, Your Highness." She straightened her inexpensive and incredibly ordinary suit jacket. "Regardless, I can see this is *not* a meeting I need to be included in, so I will take my leave."

With that she left, closing the doors with a definitive double-snick behind her.

Zahir actually smiled. "I thought Mother was a tough audience."

"Grace keeps me in line," Amir said with some humor, while he willed his libido back into check.

These moments of attraction for his indispensable assistant were coming too frequently for his comfort. But the spark in her eyes when she chastised his brother and him had lit a fire somewhere else entirely in Amir.

Zahir shook his head. "I only wish that were true." And just like that, the air of gravity was back.

"Tisa was a mistake," Amir admitted.

"Yes."

Amir refused to allow his pride to elicit offense at his brother's honesty. Tisa *had* been a mistake. In more ways than one. "Are you here on your own, or did Father send you?"

"Father sent me."

A cold fist tightened around Amir's heart. Some might think that King Faruq sending his eldest son in his place was an indication that he did not place as high of an importance on the message as he would one he delivered personally. However, Amir knew that was not true. Sending Zahir said more than Amir wanted to hear about how disappointed in him his father truly was. It implied the king was so angry, he did not even want to see his youngest son.

"You know, I realize that Tisa courts the limelight a bit too much and maybe I showed up in more than one story with her, but damn it…I never moved in with one of my flings like Khalil did with his mistress. He lived with Jade for almost two years before he decided to marry her."

And in any other universe that would have made Jade untouchable in the marriage stakes for a man in his family, but she had friends in high places. Their uncle had taken an interest in Jade and Khalil's romance and seen to it that Jade had a place in the royal family of Zorha.

Zahir's frown said how little he appreciated the reminder that his sister-in-law had been his brother's live-in lover. "Misdirection will not undo the results of your actions."

"You can assure the king that his youngest son will be more circumspect in choosing companions in future." Amir's jaw tightened against words he wanted to add, but would regret saying later.

"Unfortunately, such an assurance will not be enough. Our father has grown weary of you dragging the family name through camel dung. It is time for you to tame your wild ways permanently."

Once again, Amir had to bite back words it would be impolite to speak. But his father's and brother's attitudes grated.

He was loyal to his family and to his people. He had put the needs of each ahead of his own on more occasions than he could count. He lived away from his desert home to oversee the royal family's business interests. His position left him little time to himself and if he chose to spend that time with beautiful women in uncomplicated liaisons, how did that make him a bad person?

"I don't date innocents or married women. My companions are aware of the transitory nature of our association before I ever take them on the first date."

"So is the rest of the world."

Amir winced, but he said, "So what?"

"Your lifestyle reflects negatively on our family and our people."

"There is nothing wrong with my lifestyle."

"Our father does not agree."

"What does he want me to do, remain celibate?"

"No."

"Then what?"

A brief flash of pity flared in his eldest brother's dark eyes. "The king has decreed that you shall be married."

The king? So this was coming as a royal command. Camel dung was right. "And has he chosen my future wife?" Amir asked in disbelief.

Zahir had the grace to look at least a little uncomfortable. "Yes."

"That's positively medieval."

Again that short flicker of pity, but then Zahir's expression hardened. "Are you refusing the king's command?"

Foreboding skated up Amir's spine. He knew that to deny his father would come with a very heavy cost, maybe even his position within their family. His father almost never pulled royal rank, so when he did so, his family knew he would not be moved. If Amir refused to marry the woman his father had chosen, he might as well start looking for a new job. One that didn't have "prince" in its title.

He had been raised to do his duty and could not imagine refusing his father, unless the dictate were so untenable he could not possibly live with it. This one was not.

"I will marry the princess…. I assume the woman he's chosen is a princess."

"Actually, yes." If Zahir was surprised by his youngest brother's acquiescence, he did not show it.

"Who is it?"

"Princess Lina bin Fahd al Marwan." Zahir dropped another sheet of paper on the desk.

This one was a single-page dossier on the princess, including a picture of the beautiful woman. Maybe it wouldn't be so bad. The last thing he wanted was to marry for love and, if he was honest, he would admit that the transitory nature of the women in his life was starting to get old.

He wouldn't have chosen to marry for some time yet on his own, but he wasn't completely against the idea.

Besides, he had his own reasons for wanting a more permanent distraction than Tisa and the others like her.

"When's the wedding?" he asked.

CHAPTER ONE

"What did you say?" Grace felt like Amir had just punched her right in the solar plexus, but all he'd really done was ask her a question.

"I want you to find me a wife."

She closed her eyes and opened them again, but he was still there, her gorgeous, totally sexy, only-man-in-the-world-for-her boss. The expression of expectation on his too handsome face said he had actually made the request that she was desperately hoping had been a figment of her imagination.

Hadn't it been awful enough when he'd announced to her a mere six weeks ago that his father had decreed Amir was to marry some princess from a neighboring sheikhdom? Grace's heart had shriveled and come close to dying at how easily her usually independent and stubborn boss had so easily submitted to his father's demand.

Then a reprieve had come for Grace's bleeding emotions when Princess Lina had ended up eloping with an old flame and nullifying the contract the two powerful sheikhs had signed. That had happened almost two weeks ago and Grace was just overcoming the jagged edges of pain left by the king's edict and his youngest son's acceptance of it.

Now Amir wanted *her* to find him a wife? Just kill her now because life couldn't get much worse.

Okay, maybe it could, but even plain PAs had the right to their moments of drama.

"What? Why?" He was happy in his serial liaisons, or at least he'd always acted like he was.

Definitely, he'd never fallen in love with any of them. As far as she knew—and she knew him better than anyone else in his life, including his family—Amir had not been in love since he was eighteen years old. Not that he admitted *now* that it had been love *then*.

But she knew the signs of a true and abiding love. Didn't she live with them on a personal basis every day?

Amir had loved his Yasmine enough to ask her to marry him. They were only engaged for three months, the wedding less than a month away—which in Grace's mind showed just how much he had loved the other woman to press for such a speedy wedding—when Yasmine was killed in a freak accident. It was Grace's personal belief that the loss of his first love had impacted Amir more strongly than he ever wanted to admit to himself or his family.

But even so, this was unbelievable.

"My father wants me to settle down," Amir said with a shrug.

How could he be so blasé about this? Didn't he care that he was breaking her heart into tiny, bitty, never-to-be-put-together-again pieces? All right, so he didn't know, *but did that excuse him?* The jury was still out on that one, just like it was out on the issue of the pain he caused her regularly with his little liaisons.

"But he hasn't said anything about selecting another wife for you, has he?" she asked with desperate logic.

"No."

"So…"

"I see no reason to wait on him to do so. If you find me a wife, at least I'll have control

over the final choice and will get married on
my own terms, not his."

Grace had to stifle a groan and the urge to
smack her own forehead. She should have
expected this. Amir was far too princely to let
another man choose his wife. Now that he'd
been given a reprieve, rather than wait for his
father to exert control again, he would preempt
the king by acting on his own. She understood
the reasoning, respected it even, but no way in
the world was she going to help him.

That was simply asking too much.

"No."

His dark chocolate eyes widened almost
comically. "What do you mean no?" His
shock at her refusal was so blatant, she could
feel it like a physical presence between them.

"I mean that if you want to find a wife," she
said very slowly and very firmly, "you'll have
to do it *on your own.*"

The shock melted under his obvious dis-
content. "Don't be ridiculous. I can't make
this kind of choice without your input."

Her body jerked as if the words were
knives directed at her heart rather than the
backhanded compliment Amir intended them
to be. "I'm not being anything of the sort.

I'm your personal assistant, not a match-maker. Finding wives is not even remotely in my job description."

"That's exactly right. Your title is *personal* assistant, not *administrative* assistant, because you help me with more than just business."

"The selection of a wife is way too personal."

"No, it isn't. You've picked out gifts for my companions, how is this any different?"

"How can you ask me that?" She loved this man more than her own life, but sometimes he was so dense she was tempted to question the obscenely high IQ level he was purported to have.

Amir leaned his hip against her desk and crossed his arms, a sure sign he was settling in for the siege. "We're just arguing in circles here, Grace. I need your help."

"No. I won't do it." She would never survive it.

It hurt enough to love him like she did and know there was no chance between the two of them, but to be forced to find a woman to hold the place she wanted more than anything? That was too much. Much, much too much.

"Come on, Grace. Don't let me down now. I'll make it worth your while."

That was all she needed, the promise of a bonus for doing the one thing she never, ever, ever—not in a million years—wanted to do.

"No."

Before he could continue the argument, the phone rang and Grace leapt for it like a drowning victim going for a lifeline. When she managed to drag the call out past a minute, Amir's natural impatience got the better of him and he pushed away from her desk.

The look he gave her over his shoulder said he wasn't finished with their discussion.

Amir paced his office. What was the matter with Grace? She'd been acting strangely ever since his father had insisted he marry. At first he'd thought it was because she was worried she'd lose her job when he took a wife, but he'd assured her the opposite was true. He couldn't imagine trying to function without his insightful and efficient PA.

She'd continued to act oddly and had only settled down in the last couple of weeks— since the marriage plans with Princess Lina had fallen through.

Try as he might though, he didn't understand why Grace was balking at finding him a wife. She didn't approve of his lifestyle any more than his father did. She'd made that clear enough, though she'd never gone as far as the king and suggested Amir resort to marriage.

He would think she'd *want* input into choosing the woman that would play a key role in her life. As his PA, Grace would no doubt find herself conferring with the woman Amir married in order to arrange schedules and the like. In fact, he would expect her to help select his spouse's personal assistant so the two would work together seamlessly.

Grace had to know this wasn't something he wanted, or even felt qualified, to do alone. She understood what he needed, often before he did. She would be able to find the best candidates to fill the role to complement his life.

He wasn't looking for love, but he didn't want a wife who didn't fit in with the lifestyle he was most comfortable living. Grace understood the sheikh under the Western clothing. She understood how important his family and home were to him, even if he lived in Manhattan and reveled in his New York existence.

He thought of how she had looked when he first asked her. Stunned. Totally shocked, which actually surprised him. He would have thought she would have foreseen this move on his part. She was usually much better at anticipating his actions.

She knew he didn't want his father controlling his life, even if the older man was King of Zorha. If not now, then sometime in the future, his father would come back with another parentally approved bride. Amir's only choice was to get there first. And he would have sworn Grace would realize that.

He had half expected her to have a list of suitable candidates already compiled. This intransigent refusal to help was completely out of character for her. Not to mention unacceptable.

It didn't help that Grace was kind of cute when she was startled like that. It wasn't a look he saw often and, frankly, that was probably for the best. He couldn't afford to ruin the most important relationship with a female that he had in his life for sex.

His mother might be hurt to know he placed Grace above her—and everyone else—in importance, but there was no contest. His PA impacted his reality in both big and small ways on a daily basis. No one had more influence on his day-by-day existence than she did.

Unfortunately, she was not the type of woman he could have a fling with and then go back to his normal life. Or he would have scratched this particular itch a long time ago. And he wouldn't have ended up with Tisa, either, thus preventing the subsequent edict by his father. Regardless, he recognized that working together afterward would be impossible.

He refused to risk something as important as his relationship with his perfect-for-him personal assistant for something as ephemeral as sex.

The fact that his desire to experience that side of his dowdy assistant was getting stronger all the time only enhanced his certainty that finding a convenient wife was the best course of action for him. Which meant he had to convince Grace to help him.

They both needed the protection. Because he knew that Grace would be far too easy to persuade into his bed. She watched him with an innocent hunger that had caused him to hide more than one hard-on behind his desk. He'd long since stopped questioning why a woman so unaware of—and poor at—showcasing her feminine attributes would affect him this way.

He simply accepted that he craved pulling her long, curly mop from its tight bun and running his fingers through the red silk.

He also wanted to expose and taste the expanse of her alluring skin…the light dusting of freckles looked like sweet spice on the untouched creaminess. Did those delectable little dots cover her whole body? Were her delicious-looking apple-shaped breasts adorned with the cinnamon-looking specks?

Damn it. He had to stop thinking like this or he was going to have to start taking mid-afternoon showers…of the cold variety.

He must convince Grace to help him find a convenient wife…the only kind he wanted.

Memories of the one emotional entanglement of his life and its aftermath sent chills through his heart. No love. No intense emotional connections. He was never going there again. Not in his mind, not in his heart and definitely not in his life.

Grace settled into her seat beside Amir at Fenway Park. They'd flown to Boston on business and he had surprised her with front-row tickets to see her favorite baseball team. She loved the Boston Red Sox and any other time would be absolutely ecstatic over his generosity. Only she had a bad feeling they were by way of a bribe.

He hadn't said another word about her finding him a wife in almost a week, but she was too smart to think he'd forgotten about it. That wasn't Amir's way. She'd worked with him for five years and couldn't think of a single instance when he had ever given up something he wanted after only one argument. He was much too confident and strong-willed to be easily dissuaded from a path he'd chosen.

And he'd made it clear he wanted her on that path, choosing with him.

This wasn't right. Or even remotely fair. She should be enjoying the game. Instead, her mind was whirling with ways to convince Amir she meant business and fears that she wouldn't be able to hold the line against him.

It was hard saying no to the man you loved, even if he saw you as a piece of handy office furniture.

Amir looked sideways at her. "Everything all right?"

"Yes. I'm really happy to be here. Thank you."

The smile he flashed her was both sincere and incredibly sexy. "I am glad. And you are welcome. You deserve much more."

Okay, so not a piece of office furniture. Guilt suffused her. She sighed. She'd be willing to bet that if asked, Amir would not only describe her as a top-notch personal assistant, but he would also claim they were friends, too. And they were. The truth was, Sheikh Amir bin Faruq al Zorha was her best friend. She was pretty sure he considered her the same or close to it.

The problem for her was that she longed to be more than his friend and knew that could never happen. He was so far out of her league, she might as well be considered a player in peewees, while he was definitely a top player in the major leagues.

None of which was anything new to her, so why was she allowing the situation to ruin her current experience? The answer was, she wasn't going to. This was a wonderful treat for an obsessive baseball fan like her and she wasn't going to diminish it with depressing, but old and familiar thoughts.

Grace forced her attention back to the

men on the field. And if her senses were more in tune with the man beside her, no one had to know.

Amir had been biding his time before approaching Grace again about the issue of finding him a wife. Whatever had caused her to be less than receptive the first time around would no doubt get better with time.

This strategy had worked before. He would put an idea to Grace and give her time to think about it. If her first reaction was negative, more often than not she would talk herself into it more effectively than he could. *Usually.* He was hoping this was one of those times. But if it wasn't, he'd taken care to soften her up with a trip to Fenway Park and was in the process of buying her a team jersey after a rousing win by her favorite team.

She'd chosen one that was made for men and obviously at least a couple of sizes too big. When he'd pointed out one that would have been more formfitting, she'd shaken her head.

He couldn't complain about her propensity to wear either shapeless or oversized clothing— or both—because it was one of her habits that helped him control the frustrating desire that plagued him around her. Though even that habit was rather endearing.

He had never known a woman so clueless regarding her feminine appeal, or how to showcase it.

For this small mercy, he could only be grateful.

He waited until they were in the limo before broaching the subject on his mind and in the end, she made it easy for him.

She settled back against the leather seat facing him. "Okay, what gives? As if I didn't know."

He poured her a glass of lime Perrier and himself a finger of vodka. Too bad she did not drink. Enhancing her malleability right now could only improve his cause. "If you already know, there's no point in me saying it."

She took the sparkling water. "Thank you."

He inclined his head.

She took a sip, regarding him over the rim of her crystal tumbler.

"Thank you also for not denying that tonight has all been about buttering me up."

Now that stung. "Do you really think so?"

She just shrugged, her hair for once not

pulled up in a tight bun, but barely confined in a wild ponytail that made her look younger than her twenty-five years. She was dressed in a Red Sox T-shirt he'd bought her the year before and a pair of jeans that made her legs look a mile long. Thank goodness they were in her typical baggy style.

He gave her a chiding look. "You're not being fair, Gracey. And that's not like you."

She pouted, her lip protruding adorably, and he had to slam down on the urge to kiss her.

"Oh, all right…it's not all about buttering me up. Even if you didn't have something you wanted, you probably would have arranged tickets for the game." She rolled her eyes. "And bought me the jersey, which I'm sleeping in for the foreseeable future…so, thank you."

The image of Grace in bed was not one he could afford, so he thrust it from his mind with ruthless precision.

"I might have gotten regular box seats." Though he wasn't stingy with her and she knew it.

Grace had few passions and baseball was one of them. He indulged her as much as possible. An excellent PA like her deserved a few perks.

"Maybe…but regardless, I know you aren't above using my good mood and sense of gratitude toward you for your own ends right now."

"If I were above it as you say, I wouldn't be a very good negotiator, would I?"

"I suppose not." She bit her bottom lip and looked out the window for several seconds of silence.

"What is holding your interest? It is simply the clogged traffic we encounter after every one of these events I've taken you to."

She sighed and turned her attention back to him, her hazel eyes troubled. "You want me to find you a wife."

"Yes." He had her, he knew it. And no, he didn't feel the least guilty for getting her in a moment of weakness.

She glared at him. "You think you've won, but you haven't."

"I will."

Her frown grew more fierce, but she didn't deny it.

"If you really wanted my cooperation, you should have arranged for me to meet Big

Papi." Her eyes glowed with something that disturbed him on many levels.

"I have no desire to introduce you to your hero. Sports stars like him could benefit from having a good personal assistant, too. I will not lose you so easily." He said the words as a joke, but felt them deeply.

"You think so? I'll have to keep that in mind."

"I am not amused." The idea of her leaving him to work for the Red Sox's lauded designated hitter filled him with annoyance, even though he knew it was in no way possible.

She laughed, but then sobered almost instantly.

"I'm not saying I'm going to do it, but if I did, what are you looking for in a wife?"

The question caught him unaware, though it shouldn't have. He opened his mouth and closed it again immediately. Nothing came instantly to his normally agile brain.

She stared at him, the knowledge in her eyes growing. "You've got no idea, do you?"

"That's why I asked you."

"But Amir, this is *your* wife we're talking about. I can't just make a list of candidates and ask you to choose."

"Why not?"

"Because you have to tell me what you want first!" For some reason, her agitation made him feel better.

"You know what I want." Probably better than he did.

"You were happy with your father's choice."

"All but the fact that it was his choice, that is true." Was that pain that chased so quickly across her features? She had no reason to be hurt. It must be the subdued lighting in the limo playing tricks on him. "I prefer to pick out my own wife," he said when she did not respond.

"Then why are you demanding I do it?"

"It's different, and you know it. Now stop being difficult."

"I'm not the difficult one. How can you possibly expect me to do what you ask without giving me some guidelines in which to work?"

"Fine. She needs to be physically attractive."

"Is that all?" Grace asked with a sarcasm few could match.

"No. She has to be cultured and diplomatic."

"I see." Her formerly animated attitude had become subdued.

Was his lack of helpfulness bothering her that much? "I want to marry a woman who will complement me and my position, both in the business world and within the political realm when I am operating within my role as sheikh-slash-prince."

"I got that."

"Oh."

She sighed.

"I'm not sure what you mean by attractive."

"Are you being deliberately obtuse?" He would not put it past her. His PA could be very stubborn and going passive-aggressive was not outside of her repertoire.

"You think so? You once said you did not see what made Jade so special for Khalil. Obviously, you two have differing tastes. Most people do."

"But you know the type of woman that attracts me. You've seen and spoken with— hell, you've shopped for—the women I've dated."

"But one must assume these women lack something, or you would have married one of them by now."

"I am ready to marry. Perhaps if I had been before, I would be married to one of my former companions."

"But you never loved any of them."

"I don't plan to love my wife, either. This is a marriage of convenience."

"So, then what difference does it make if your future wife is attractive, or not?"

"Now you are being naive. A beautiful wife can only benefit me."

"You mean like a trophy wife."

"I mean like a feminine companion that will add to my *éclat*, not detract from it."

"That is so shallow."

"It is realistic."

"Whatever."

He had disappointed her…again. She was very good at her job, but still very innocent to the ways of the world. He decided to explain in a way that might embarrass her, but would not offend her sense of fairness.

"I do not wish the need to remain faithful to become a purgatory for me, either."

"So, you plan to be?"

"Faithful? Yes, of course. The men in my family are not philanderers."

"Everything you have listed up to now is superficial…what about you and she having interests, likes and dislikes in common?"

"Not necessary. It's not even preferred. As long as we are compatible in bed, we can lead totally separate lives."

She looked at him as if she questioned his

sanity, which was frankly a marginal improvement over her doubting his integrity.

"That's not the best environment to raise children in, or didn't you plan to be a father?"

"I do not have to be a besotted fool to be a good father."

"Your parents love each other."

"So?"

"Are you saying you don't want that for yourself and your family? Not even a little?"

Thoughts of the only time he had ever known anything close bombarded his brain, leading to memories of Yasmine.

During the time right after Yasmine died, his mind shied away from those images, and the pain and weakness they represented. "Not everyone craves that kind of relationship. I definitely do not."

Her frown was back full force. "With an attitude like that, it would serve you right if I did it."

"That's exactly what I'm hoping."

But she wasn't listening, or at least she wasn't looking at him. She was too busy glaring out the window again. What was her problem?

Was it possible his ultra-efficient secretary who dressed dowdily and never dated had a severely hidden but equally deep romantic streak? It would certainly explain her negative reaction to his proposed marriage of convenience…both the one his father had decreed and the one Amir himself was trying to facilitate with her help.

It would also explain why she never dated. Because no matter how dowdily she dressed, he knew other men had to have noticed the latent sensuality in his Grace. But apparently she was waiting for Mr. Right…the knight in shining armor to come along and sweep her off her feet. In a way, he was glad she had this hidden streak of romanticism. It kept her working by his side rather than off dating and/or married to another man.

"Will you just think about it, Grace?" He played the card she'd never been able to ignore in the past. "Please."

Her gaze slid to him, another expression he could not read settled in her hazel eyes. "Okay, I'll think about it."

Victory was his, if he just waited.

Something of his certainty must have shown on his face because she pursed her lips with affront. "Don't look so smug. I may yet say no."

It was so unlikely as to be an impossibility, but he was savvy enough to her ways not to say so.

CHAPTER TWO

GRACE CURLED UP on the sofa in the living area of the two-bedroom suite she and Amir shared, pretending to watch an old Hepburn-Tracy movie on low volume. But all she was really doing was thinking about Amir.

He'd once told her that if his family knew of their traveling arrangements, it would upset his mother. In the next breath, he had laughed as if the idea of anything inappropriate happening between them was too funny for words.

And wasn't it?

She'd asked him what constituted attractive to him and he had pointed her to his former playmates after agreeing he had been perfectly happy with his father's choice for his future wife. Every one of those women fell in the realm of near physical perfection. He dated models, but usually stuck to women within his social set, women who dressed like they should be on the cover of a fashion magazine even if they weren't. And Princess Lina. She was a pocket Venus if there ever was one. Grace's hands went to her own small breasts and she frowned.

If she had to be as tall as a lot of men, couldn't she have gotten the voluptuous curves to go with her height? Instead she was stick-skinny with what could charitably be called understated curves. Hugging the throw pillow from the sofa, she frowned. Amir had said not one word about personality or compatibility, unless she wanted to count sex. Was he really that shallow?

She knew he wasn't. So why was he willing to settle for a marriage of convenience with a woman who had little more to offer than her beauty and ability to be charming in social situations? He deserved so much more. His passionate soul *needed* more, even if he refused to see it.

This had to be the result of losing Yasmine at such a young age. He'd once told her the grief had led him places he never wanted to go back to. The men of the Zorhan royal family hated any semblance of weakness. Perhaps Amir even more than the others, because he was the youngest and felt he had something to prove.

It must have been difficult growing up an alpha male with two brothers of equally dominant natures. She often saw him chafing against that reality even now. But to resort to this? It wasn't right.

The *second to the last* thing Grace ever wanted to see was Amir in love with another woman. The *last* was him married to a woman he could never love. As annoyed as his current attitude made her, she couldn't help wanting him to be happy.

He wasn't going to end up that way married to some empty-headed beauty, who shared nothing in common with him but her ability to traverse the two worlds he inhabited and her prowess in bed.

Grace hugged the pillow more tightly, feeling lonelier than she had since first meeting Amir. From the moment she'd walked into his office at the age of twenty to interview for the position of personal assistant, he had changed her world. He'd filled it with light, warmth and sound.

The social awkwardness that usually plagued her did not touch her when she was

with him. It was as if, standing in his shadow
in her role as PA, she was part of him. He
had nothing to be shy and awkward about
and therefore neither did she on his behalf.
She had felt at home in his office from the
very beginning.

She'd also loved him practically from the
first, not that she'd realized it. Sure, it had
started as a typical crush on the gorgeous,
wealthy prince—and even when she'd had a
crush on him, she'd been singularly naive to
what that meant. But Amir had quickly
shown her that he was more than a rich and
pretty face.

He cared about his family. He cared about
the people of Zorha. He cared about the
people of his adopted home, giving more to
charities than most businessmen ever dreamed
of doing. He was also kind to children and old
people. It was such a cliché, but true. Not to
mention, he was patient and generous toward
his nondescript PA. Not patient and generous
enough to consider her for the position of his
convenient wife though.

For a mad moment, right at first, she had
let herself imagine it was possible.

After all, hadn't he made a point of saying

he didn't expect or even want to love his future wife? Even the idea that his wife must be able to move in his different worlds had fit Grace. She might have spent her entire life until she came to work for him being socially backward and tongue-tied in any situation that included more than two people, but she'd found her niche with him and learned to function as his personal assistant no matter where they were or who they were with.

Couldn't she have done the same as his wife?

Oh, sure, she mocked herself. Grace Brown, future princess. She could just see it. Not.

Ignoring the hot wetness tracking down her cheeks, she replayed the moment in the limo when she'd realized she could never put herself forward as a candidate for him to consider. Right up to that second, she'd still been harboring secret, crazy fantasies. Only when he had said he wanted to be attracted to his bride—so his vows of faithfulness did not create a purgatory for him to live in—had she known. One thing Grace was absolutely certain of, Amir did not want her sexually.

It was as that reality came home to her that her ill-conceived dreams shattered around her, leaving her already battered heart hemorrhaging.

Now, she sat, unable to sleep, considering what the future held for her. Pain. Yes. She saw no way around it. The man she loved with every fiber of her being was going to marry another woman. If she loved him enough and was strong enough, she was going to help him find that woman.

Why?

Because it was the one chance she had to ensure as much of Amir's future personal happiness as she could. If she continued to refuse to help him, he would end up marrying some beautiful icicle and think that was exactly what he wanted because it did not put his heart at risk.

Grace was not a fool, at least not a complete one. She knew he was avoiding any chance of being weak like he had been when he was eighteen. He did not want to hurt and she understood that. What *he* didn't understand was that loneliness within his marriage would chip away at his warm heart until it was as cold as he thought he wanted it to be.

She could not stand the prospect of such a thing happening to him. The only way she could help him avoid it was to find him a convenient wife that had the potential to be so much more.

If her own heart lost the final fight in the process, she would survive…somehow.

Amir sat down to the breakfast Grace had ordered them. Dark circles painted the skin below her eyes and her skin was even more pale than normal.

He frowned, concern making his voice edgy. "You look tired. Didn't you sleep well last night? Are you coming down with something?"

"I'm not sick, but I didn't sleep much, either." She smiled, a muted facsimile of her usual expression.

"Because of what I asked you to do?"

"Yes."

"If it causes you such concern, I withdraw my request." He did not want her losing sleep over this project. She worked too hard as it was. She had no more of a life outside his business than he did.

"That won't be necessary."

"What do you mean?"

"I decided to take on the assignment."

"But if it makes you like this…" His words

trailed off, but he swept his hand toward her, leaving no doubt what he was talking about. "You look terrible."

She grimaced. "Thank you so much, Amir."

"This is no time for false modesty. Are you sure you are not ill?"

"I am positive. I am also certain that I am willing to help you find a wife."

Something inside him jolted, but he ignored it. "That is a relief."

She smiled, this one more genuine. "I'm glad."

"Thank you, but I do not want you making yourself sick. Tell me if it is too much."

She laughed. "Right. Like you won't be demanding the list in twenty-four hours."

"I am not that impatient."

"Yes, you are." But humor, not irritation, laced her voice.

Gratitude for her surged through him and he found himself standing up and walking around the table to pull her into a rare hug.

At first, she stood in rigid shock in his embrace, but then she relaxed, clinging to him. Her warm feminine body pressed tightly to his and inescapable arousal surged through him.

He did not let go.

She did not step away.

His head tipped down of its own volition as he instinctively sought to take in more of her scent. "You smell like cinnamon," he said against her yet-to-be-put-up mass of red curls. "And jasmine." The fragrance reminded him of home.

"Your mother sends me handmade soaps and hair products from her herbalist." Grace's face was buried in his neck and her voice came out a husky whisper.

He lifted his head and then tilted her chin up with his finger until their eyes met. "My mother sends you things?"

"Yes. Since after our first trip to Zorha when I remarked that I loved the soaps and shampoos I found in the palace baths."

"She likes you." He wondered why he had never noticed that before. Perhaps because he assumed others would like her. There was nothing unlikable about Grace. She could be shy and stubborn even, but she was not annoying.

"I like her, too."

"It pleases me that you do." She worked too close with him for it to be comfortable for anyone involved if she did not. Why hadn't he let Grace go yet? This hug was becoming something more, something he could not afford for it to become. He willed himself to step back, but his arms remained stubbornly around her. Now that she was looking up at him, her lips were an enticing few inches from his. They parted, her delicious-looking pink tongue just barely visible.

Her breathing increased and if he looked down and drew her suit jacket away, he knew he would see hardened nipples. Her response to his presence was one reason it had become so difficult to fight his own desires. He didn't do it. He had that much sanity left.

She was strangely silent, very unlike his Grace.

Even in her sensible inch-and-a-half heels, she was taller than most of the women he dated. Tall enough to be just the right height for him to tilt his head slightly and be kissing her. The temptation was growing by the second and her hazel eyes going dark and unfocused with desire were not helping.

She wanted him, but it was the desire of the innocent. She did not know how it would end. She was not one of his women. Grace was a far more permanent fixture in his life and he intended to keep it that way.

But right now, the temptation to taste that innocence was overwhelming.

His PDA's alarm went off, reminding him of an upcoming meeting at the same time that Grace's started beeping from the other room.

The interruption of the discordant beeping was what he needed to find the wherewithal to let her go and step back. "Potential candidates should probably be taller than the princess. You fit well in my arms."

He couldn't believe he'd said anything so easily misconstrued, but Grace didn't look triumphant.

Rather, her expression became carefully neutral as she turned away. "I'll make a note of it."

As she left to retrieve her electronic diary and briefcase, Amir castigated himself for coming so close to disaster. What was he thinking? Why had he hugged her when he was on such a sexual edge? Others might look at his no-nonsense assistant and think she was anything but seductive. Amir knew better. He knew just how dangerous the sweet innocent was.

And for that reason alone, he deserved the painful erection in his trousers and the sexual frustration he would be feeling long after it subsided. He knew better than to do something so stupid as to hug her.

If he had kissed Grace, it would have led inevitably to bedding her.

And then losing her.

She was too valuable a PA and friend to do something that idiotic.

This whole marriage thing needed to happen quickly.

Grace tried not to stare at Amir as he spoke to the software developer about investing in the man's company. It was harder than it usually was. For one thing, she'd done her research. This was a good deal only a fool would pass up and her boss was anything but a fool. But for another, she kept getting sidetracked by the way his designer sportcoat fit his muscular body. Which, for whatever weird associative reason, kept taking her mind back to what had happened earlier in the hotel room.

The problem was, she still wasn't sure what *had* happened.

Had he almost kissed her? It had certainly seemed like it. He'd definitely held her longer than your average hug between employer and employee. Did other employers hug their personal assistants? Certainly, Amir did not do so often. The last time had been her birthday two years ago. Why had he hugged her? At first she'd thought he was saying thank-you for agreeing to help him, but did a thank-you hug last that long? Did the hug fall under their "friendship?"

And if so, why do it now? Why not before he'd asked her to find another woman for him to marry?

But what she really wanted to know, thought she might die if she didn't figure out was: *had he almost kissed her?*

Was the hardness against her stomach a figment of her imagination or irrefutable proof that as impossible as it might seem, *she turned him on?* Or was she sliding into mad dreams again that were going to leave her crushed in their wake as any other she had woven around her too captivating employer? He'd pushed her away with further requirements about his future wife. Perhaps he had only held Grace that long to test the theory that he would prefer a tall woman. Most of the women he dated were at least two inches shorter than Grace's five foot nine.

How incredibly demoralizing if that was indeed the case. Then, what could be more lowering than to be asked by the man you were crazy in love with to help him find his future bride?

"Grace?"

Her head snapped up at the impatient tone in Amir's voice. Both men were looking at her.

"Did you get that?"

Heat climbing into her cheeks, she had to admit she hadn't and asked the other man to repeat himself. That was so unlike her efficient self, she knew she'd hear about it later from the sheikh. Jerry, the software developer, was awfully nice about it, smiling at her and asking very politely if she'd gotten it all the second time around. She found herself relaxing under his kindness and responded a bit more warmly than was her usual wont. She had a feeling they were going to end up being friends. She was sure she would have lots of opportunities to interact with him as she would be the liaison to Amir.

"It's too bad you are headquartered here," she said without thought.

"Or that the sheikh's office *isn't* here," Jerry said without missing a beat.

"I do not see either as a tragedy." Amir's tone was frosty and Grace had to stifle a sigh.

She smiled apologetically at Jerry. "He's still angry I wasn't paying attention just now."

"*He* does not appreciate being spoken about as if *he* were not sitting right beside you."

"My apologies." Jerry looked worried, so Grace did not say what was on the tip of her tongue.

In fact, she didn't say anything.

A few minutes later, when Jerry and Amir were making plans to share dinner and a drink to celebrate the deal, he asked if Grace would be joining them. Before she could get a word in edgewise, Amir said she had things to work on and wouldn't be able to.

She couldn't believe his effrontery and was ready to blast him the minute they got to the privacy of their suite, but Jerry had already dealt with enough of her boss's crankiness.

As soon as the door shut, she whirled on him. "What exactly is so pressing that I'm supposed to be skipping dinner to work on it?"

He glared at her. "You have agreed to find me a wife. Have you forgotten already?"

"I'm not headed toward dementia yet, though goodness knows working with you will send me there early."

"What is that supposed to mean?"

"It means that I find it beyond rude that you turned down a dinner invitation on my behalf simply because you think I should spend my off-hours working on your pet project."

"You've never minded putting in over-time before."

"You've never dictated when it should happen, and for your information, I had no intention of starting the great wife hunt tonight."

"Are you saying you want to have dinner with Jerry?"

"I thought that was obvious."

"Maybe I should just stay here and let the two of you make a night out on the town of it."

Had he lost his mind? "What in the world are you talking about?"

"You and Jerry. You appear to have gotten quite chummy."

"You're basing this on the fact I wanted to eat dinner with you?"

"You were flirting with him."

"I *never* flirt." She had no idea how.

"You *smiled*."

"And that is a crime now? You were smiling, too."

"I most assuredly was *not* flirting."

She took a deep breath and tried another tack. "Name the last business dinner I did not accompany you to."

"Last month, when I had dinner with Sandor Christofides regarding using his ships for importation of certain goods to Zorha."

This was getting beyond ridiculous. "I was in Seattle setting up for your arrival at the business conference!"

"You made no stipulation of where you were at the time…you simply told me to name the last dinner you had missed. So I did. Now, I expect you to work on my project."

"I'll work on it when I decide to work on it, and that is not going to be tonight when I could be having a pleasant dinner with a business associate."

"He is *my* business associate."

"What is the matter with you? You've never acted this way about me sharing dinner with you and an associate before."

Wasn't it bad enough he was planning to marry another woman, was he trying to ease Grace out of other areas of his life as well?

"I did not like the way Jerry looked at you."

"*What?* Like he pitied me for having such a churlish boss?"

Amir drew himself up and positively glowered. "I am not churlish."

"Dismissing me from your dinner plans without a by-your-leave certainly doesn't constitute polite behavior."

"So, we are back to that."

"We never left it," she said with exasperation.

"We are leaving it now."

"And that leaves *me* where?"

He had enough sense to look chagrined. "Would you like me to call and cancel so you will not be forced to eat alone?"

She was not a charity case. She might have been shy and backward when she first came to work for Amir, but she'd grown a lot in five years. "Of course not, then Jerry would consider you inconsistent and that is hardly the impression you want to give a business associate."

"So, you will stay here and work on my personal project."

"No. I will find my own dinner out there." She pointed out the window. "I will no doubt return far too late to work on anything. Now if you will excuse me, I need to change into something besides business attire."

It was her turn not to give him a chance to answer as she marched into her bedroom, making mental plans for the evening as she went.

Amir stood in dumb transfixion as he listened to the silence left behind after Grace's door slammed shut. "I would prefer a wife who does not slam doors," he said loudly into the empty room.

The sound of another door, this one Grace's bathroom, shutting with noisy force was his only answer.

Damn it. What had happened? One minute he had been closing a lucrative deal and the next he was verbally fencing with a termagant. Had she been serious about going out on her own? Perhaps not as active as New York, Boston nevertheless had a distinct nightlife. And Grace planned to participate in it?

Never!

It was time for a trip home where the only

nightlife was listening to the nocturnal sounds in the desert. Yes, definitely…he and Grace needed to go to Zorha. He could meet with his father and brothers and discuss their new business ventures while she cajoled his mother into sending her more fragrant soaps.

What to do about tonight? Clearly he had two options. He could include her in the dinner with Jerry, who had spent the latter part of their meeting all but drooling over Amir's dowdy assistant. Had the man no taste…or was he more discerning than most? Amir feared the latter. He feared even more that Jerry saw Grace as an easy mark and that she would prove to be one. She was ripe to be plucked from the tree of her virginity.

His other option was to allow her to go out for an evening on her own. In her current frame of mind, she was likely to do something she would regret later. As her friend, he was conscience-bound not to allow that. At least if she came with him to dinner, he could keep an eye on her.

And if Jerry thought he would be taking Grace home for a nightcap, he had a rude awakening ahead of him.

CHAPTER THREE

GRACE ADJUSTED her seat belt and looked out the window of the private jet at the wet tarmac. It was raining. Nothing new about that in New York in the spring. At least that was one good thing about heading to the desert. No dreary, gray days ahead. But other than the improvement in weather, she did not understand *why* they were headed to Zorha.

"Tell me again why we are going home?"

Amir said nothing about her slip of the tongue, though technically, they were headed to *his* home, not hers. Grace's home was a four-bedroom farmhouse in upstate New York. She still marveled at the fact that the former farmgirl, who had taken a two-year course in office management at a college near the city, had ended up a prince's personal assistant.

"Amir?"

He turned to face her, his dark brown eyes reflecting a question. "Yes?"

"What are you thinking about so hard that you didn't hear me?"

"I am always like this before going home. I am thinking of all that I miss and all that I will be happy to see."

She smiled. "Is that why we're traveling to see your family two full months ahead of our scheduled trip? You're homesick?"

Something odd passed over his gorgeous face, but it was quickly gone. "It is part of it."

"What is the other part, if you don't mind telling me?"

"I do."

"What? You mind?" The knot that had formed in her stomach the day she'd learned his father wanted him to marry a princess got tighter. Just as she'd feared in Boston, Amir was pushing her out of his life in small, but significant ways. "I see. Well, never mind then. Um…I'll just work on my report for your father."

"Your report for my father?"

"Yes. He wanted more information on the shipping deal. I mentioned that to you….you said it was fine if I wrote the report. Have you changed your mind?"

"No, of course not. I had forgotten, that is all."

"That's not like you."

"I have had some things on my mind."

Probably more things he did not want to talk about, so she didn't make the mistake this time of asking.

"Perhaps we could go over the candidates you have found for my project."

It felt funny talking about his future wife as a project, but Amir had taken an extremely businesslike view of the whole thing since the beginning, and that attitude had not wavered a single iota.

"I am not finished and I don't want to discuss it until I am."

"You said you knew I would ask for the list in twenty-four hours. It has been almost a week."

"I didn't say I would have it ready." She wasn't avoiding giving it to him for personal reasons. She *wasn't*. It just had to be right and finding women she thought would suit him and were worthy of him was no easy task.

"Perhaps if you spent more time on it than showing Jerry around New York."

She hadn't been surprised when Amir had arranged for her to have dinner with the two men that night in Boston, but she had only agreed to go because Jerry was expecting her. She had still been very angry with her boss. She *had* been surprised when Jerry turned up in New York two days later.

He had an unexpected, but necessary, meeting with his graphic designer for the software packaging.

"You were with us most of the time."

"I did not have other things I needed to be doing."

"We *always* have stuff on our to-do list. The only way to manage it is to know when to take a break."

"So, you chose to take a break with Jerry."

"As did you."

Amir's mouth snapped shut on whatever he was going to say next.

"If you are that worried about the project, I'll work on it instead of the report for your father. I'm sure he'll understand and even applaud the decision."

"That will not be necessary and we will not be bringing this particular project up to him."

"Fine."

He scowled at her victorious grin. "You are ruthless."

"I learned from the best!"

Amir watched Grace doze in her seat. She had been yawning long before she finished the report for his father and closed her laptop. Learned from the best indeed. He could let his smile at her cleverness show now. Grace was one of the few people in his life who could win an argument with him.

She shifted her head and the pale bruising under her eyes became more noticeable.

She was not getting enough sleep lately. *Was* his personal project taking too much of her time? Perhaps he should ask his mother to help her, but wouldn't that be like inviting his father's advice as well? Amir wanted as much of this decision as possible to be under *his* strict control. However, if it meant Grace getting sick from lack of sleep, he would compromise.

Perhaps his mother would be willing to keep the project a secret until his choice had been made.

He was surprised Grace had not asked what things had been on his mind. It was very unlike him to have forgotten she was writing that report for his father. Possibly that was further evidence of her worn state. In a way, he was glad she had not asked though. He and Grace had spoken on most subjects in the past five years, but he wasn't willing to discuss his libido with her. Especially when it was causing him so much stress in relation to her. He needed a woman, that was all. However, between arranging the last-minute trip home and his usual business duties, he did not have time to find one.

Even a sure thing.

Besides, when he'd made noises about going clubbing on the only night they had free before flying out, Grace had made her displeasure known. She had the ridiculous opinion that since he had asked her to find him a convenient wife, he shouldn't be seen with other women right now. Her romanticism showing again.

He didn't agree, of course. However, it wasn't worth arguing about in light of her cooperation regarding the trip. His decision to go home had been precipitous and despite the fact he was her boss, she could have put up any number of roadblocks to prevent it. The most worrisome obstacle being a refusal to accompany him.

She'd never done so before, but she'd been edgy lately and he wasn't about to risk it. Besides, if he gave her a completely free night, chances were she would go out on her own. Or she would make plans to see Jerry, who had conveniently followed them up from Boston.

Knowing the man was in the city had been the final impetus Amir had needed to invite Grace out to dinner to discuss their upcoming trip, rather than going clubbing.

She was in a vulnerable place, even if she didn't realize it. She was twenty-five years old and if he didn't miss his guess—and he almost never did when it concerned his ever efficient PA—she was still completely innocent. She wouldn't realize Jerry was only looking for a night or two of entertainment before returning to Boston. She wasn't like the women Amir dated. Grace was too giving for her own good and was apt to get her heart broken, especially with that heretofore unknown streak of romanticism coloring her views.

It was Amir's job to protect her. After all, he was her boss. She was his responsibility.

She made an adorable snuffly sound and turned in her seat. Why hadn't he noticed before how cute his assistant was? He was surprised more men like Jerry hadn't come out of the woodwork in the past. Amir had known for a while he found her sexually stimulating, but she was sweet…and…and cuddly.

How very odd. Or perhaps not so odd. After all "cuddly" was not a prerequisite for an effective personal assistant. It therefore made sense he had not noticed this trait before.

The question was, why was he noticing it now?

It all went back to the fact he hadn't dated since the fiasco with Tisa. He'd broken up with her a week before his brother had come to see him, which made it eight weeks since he had sought female companionship. Crass as it sounded, even in his own brain, his libido attested to that fact.

And there was no relief in sight. The lack of nightlife in Zorha would not only keep his PA on a short leash, but it would also him as well.

There was no way he would risk conduct- ing a discreet affair under the extremely watchful eyes of his father and his brothers. He chafed at the restraints returning to his family would bring, yet anticipated seeing them at the same time.

It had always been thus.

Being the youngest in a family of throw-back dominant males—or at least that was the terminology his mother and Grace had used on his last visit—grated against his need to control his own life and at least influence the lives of those around him. There was something to be said for the way some desert kings split their rule into sheikhdoms overseen by their offspring, who ultimately submitted only to the king himself.

He supposed being sent to live in New York had been his father's way of doing the same thing. His father had sent his other brother, Khalil, off to operate as a diplomat, living in Greece. And King Faruq trained Zahir to take his place when he was gone.

Without realizing he was doing it, the whole time he'd been thinking about his father and brothers, Amir's fingertips had rested on Grace's smooth cheek. He traced the faint line of freckles and then the curve of her jaw, all the while knowing he had to stop touching.

She sighed, a soft, extremely sexy sound. Then she whispered his name and he had to fight the urge to kiss her sleep-softened lips. What was she thinking about to say his name?

CHAPTER FOUR

HE WITHDREW HIS HAND slowly, not wanting to wake her and wishing the contact was not having such a direct impact on the rapidly swelling hardness in his trousers.

"Would you like anything to drink, sir?"

Amir looked up to find the politely inquiring face of the plane steward. "A glass of Absolut."

"Yes, Your Highness."

"Sir is fine."

The younger man actually blushed. "I'm sorry, Your Highness, I should not have been so lax."

Oh, dear, his father's butler had been training the staff again.

"It does not bother me."

"I would like to keep my job all the same, Your Highness."

Amir nodded. He understood. Like too

many things in his life, this, too, was dictated by his born role. Was he happy or frustrated that he had not been born to rule? He had never been able to answer that question. The only conclusion he had come to that was even halfway satisfying, was that he did not begrudge his brother the position. Zahir would make a fine king one day.

The steward returned with a rock glass of Absolut and a tall glass of Perrier water. "She instructed I bring it if you asked for alcohol, Prince Amir," he said, indicating the sleeping Grace.

The little tyrant. But Amir did not instruct the steward to remove the water. Grace firmly believed that alcoholic consumption should always be followed by that of water or healthy juices. Who was he to argue the point? He had never had so much as a dry mouth, much less a hangover since she came to work for him.

Memories of both from the time after Yasmine died left a bitter taste in his mouth even the vodka could not dispel.

He would never risk losing himself so completely again. The partying and drinking hadn't lasted very long. Three to four months at the most, but he still remembered the

morning he had woken on the stone balus-
trade of the balcony outside his bedroom. He
had slept there—maybe passed out—for
several hours.

His room was on the second floor of the
palace, so it was not certain that if he had fallen,
he would have died. But he definitely would
have broken something, and for what? So he
could join the woman he loved in the afterlife?
He was not that melodramatic—or weak.

Love. It was not an emotion he needed. A
convenient wife would in every way be better
than risking such emotional weakness again.

Amir finished both the Absolut and the
water before leaning his seat back and
closing his eyes. The lights dimmed around
him, proving that the steward was not only
obedient to his training, but attentive.

Grace woke up to the sound of a steady
thump-thump-thump and a warm, firm pillow
under her cheek. The subtle scent of Amir's
cologne mixed with his natural essence told
her subconscious who she was snuggled up
against before her waking mind caught up.
The lights were still low and all of the
window shades had been pulled down so the

cabin was only lit with a very dim glow from emergency lights.

She allowed herself to revel in the sensation of being cuddled by her boss, knowing that soon enough she would have to pull away. She did not want him to wake with his arms around her. She had no doubts that she was leaning against him because *she* had moved in the night, not because he had pulled her into his embrace. She almost laughed at the ludicrousness of the thought.

But she held her humor in even as she managed to control her need to nuzzle his chest and take in more of his masculine aroma. She would probably never be this close again.

At least not unencumbered by his conscious perusal as she was now.

She remembered the first time she realized what the sensations she experienced around him meant. She'd never wanted a man before. She'd never dated. Not once. Not even a pity date with her cousin's boyfriend's best friend, or anything like that. So, when her heart rate had increased in Amir's presence, she'd first chalked it up to her usual nerves.

When her breathing had become more

erratic, she'd wondered if she was developing asthma. When her womb clenched and that place between her thighs that had never been touched by anyone but a doctor's clinical hand pulsed with some nameless need, she'd thought she was having muscle spasms.

She'd been mortified when she took her symptoms to the doctor only to be told by the kindly, but elderly GP that she was in lust.

She hadn't believed him, thinking he just didn't have a believable diagnosis for the things she'd been experiencing. But then, the next day, Amir had touched her…something very innocent, but it had sent all of her senses careening at once. Nerve endings she'd had no idea even existed within her had started buzzing and she'd been forced to stifle the insane urge to touch him back. Not so innocently.

Feeling like an idiot, she'd tried to read *The Joy of Sex* to figure out what was happening to her, but the book was clearly targeted toward sexually active people and she wasn't one. When she'd gotten to the chapter on light bondage, she'd about had a heart attack and slammed it shut, hidden it deep in a cabinet and never taken it out again.

Then she'd heard something another

woman said and thought she ought to try reading romances. They were much better because at least they explained the whole connection between her physical symptoms and the psychological ones she'd been having as well. In some ways, she wished she'd never picked up her first book though, because the novels also peeled away the barrier between what she was feeling and the name for it.

She was in love.

Hopelessly. Head over heels. Probably never to be repeated. Drowning in it. Love.

Amir moved in his sleep and, trying to stay boneless, Grace shifted with him. It felt so good, this closeness. She closed her eyes and memorized the sensation for the years of loneliness ahead. She knew they were coming…he was already pulling away. How long before she was no longer his friend, and maybe even no longer his PA?

Banishing the painful thoughts of her future, she breathed in the scent of her beloved, her brain imprinting the sensation of her head on his chest, her ear to his heart, her breasts pressed to his side. If only this moment could last forever.

He moved again, his hand grazing down her back and settling against her hip. It felt so good. So *right*. Didn't he know she belonged here, in his arms? But of course he didn't because it was only in her heart, her fantasies, that this was the way things were supposed to be. And if she didn't move soon, things could get very embarrassing for her.

Very carefully, she pulled back, returning to her seat completely. She leaned in the opposite direction, against the cold bulkhead...the loneliness that was her life and her life to come settling around her like a funeral shroud.

Amir woke, fully alert as always. Grace was still sleeping beside him, her head against the wall of the plane. It didn't look like a comfortable position so he gently adjusted her until she was leaning back in her seat, with one of the small pillows they'd been given earlier resting under her cheek.

He shook his head at the steward, who was asking with hand motions if Amir wanted the lights raised. They had forty-five minutes before they would land, so he saw no reason to waken Grace before absolutely necessary. She needed her rest.

Fifteen minutes later, he allowed the lights to be turned on and asked quietly that tea be prepared for Grace while coffee was prepared for him.

The smell of the fragrant brew made Grace's nose wrinkle…then her eyelids fluttered…then opened. She smiled, not quite awake, her hazel gaze filled with an emotion he did not recognize and had no desire to name. "Hello, Amir."

"Hello to you, too."

She sat up, seeming to wake up more completely as she did so, and the open warmth on her face faded as the pillow he had placed under her cheek fell away. "Did I sleep long?"

"Several hours actually, but I slept for part of them as well."

"I know."

"You must have woken during the night. You usually do on these flights."

"Yes." Then, unaccountably, she blushed.

He frowned. "Is something the matter?"

"Nothing that a cup of hot tea won't cure," she said with what looked like a forced smile.

"I have asked the steward to prepare it."

"Thank you."

"I must take care of you, you belong to me."

She laughed, though her eyes reflected a sadness he did not understand. "This is not the Dark Ages, Amir. A sheikh's employee is not his personal responsibility or property. I don't belong to you."

He did not agree, but forbore arguing. After all, her words were rational; his feelings were not, but as she said, he had centuries of attitude to overcome.

Grace followed Amir into the private dining room of the Royal Palace in Zorha. While the room was used for meals for the royal family and only their closest friends, it was far from modest. It might not be even a quarter the size of the corresponding formal room, but it was every bit as luxuriously appointed. The teak floors were done in an intricate design that created a natural placement for the large circular marble table in the center.

King Faruq said that when the family dined together, no issue needed to be made of whose place was at the head of the table.

His opinion was deceptively egalitarian, but Grace knew better. The fact was, the king expected his sons not to have to be reminded of his position as top dog because they were unshakably aware of it. Nevertheless, she'd always found the oldest member of the royal family surprisingly likable.

In some ways, he even reminded her of her own father, a man who ruled *his* family with the same sense of entitlement, if not royal right. Both men cared deeply for their families, too.

Her father had seen how unhappy Grace was in her life in the small town she'd been raised in. He'd pretty much forced her to go to the city to take the business course. She hadn't wanted to, her shyness rearing its ugly head again. But her dad had simply put his foot down and Grace was no more capable of defying him outright than any of her other siblings. She'd thanked him later, though.

More than once.

He'd simply said it was good to see her happy and being the woman he had always known she could be. Her mom was a lot more emotional about it. The first time they'd seen Grace after she started working for Amir, the older woman had cried. With happiness. She'd said that it was the only time in her life, she'd seen Grace confident in herself.

Grace didn't know why she'd been such a

shy kid, or why even now when she went home, she tended to shrink back into her shell at first. It was only at first though, which showed she'd grown as much as her father had thought she would…and should. Whatever.

Maybe her introverted nature had been the result of standing out in ways that made her feel self-conscious rather than unique. She'd always been taller than the other kids, even the boys until her last couple of years in high school. And her bright red hair that curled too much to be tamed made her easy to pick out in a crowd, no matter how big it was. Maybe it was simply being the second to the youngest in a family of eight children. She'd not been the baby and she'd never seen herself as anything special.

Her sisters and brothers were all talented in different ways, but until Grace met Amir she hadn't known she could be someone special, too. Coordinating both his business and a big chunk of the prince's personal life was nothing to be dismissed as trivial though. It was anything but. If Grace made a mistake, millions of dollars could be lost or a country's government offended. She didn't make mistakes though. And that felt good.

Grace's thoughts had taken her through entering the dining room and sitting beside Amir's mother.

Queen Adara smiled. "It is a pleasure to see you again, Grace."

"Thank you, Your Highness. It's good to be back in Zorha."

"I am glad you think so. Amir loves his home."

Grace allowed a servant to place a linen napkin in her lap. "It is too bad he cannot live here full-time."

Adara nodded. "But it is the way of things. My husband wisely realizes that his sons would not thrive as they must if all three spent their lives permanently in our homeland."

"And because Amir was born last rather than first, he must be exiled to another country for most of the time?" Grace wasn't sure where the question had come from.

She certainly had no desire to offend the queen. It was just that she knew Amir would rather live in the desert, among his people, than New York, no matter how much he enjoyed the busy pace of life there.

Far from looking offended, Queen Adara's expression was one of warm approval. "He is lucky to have an assistant so loyal to him."

"I'm the lucky one. I love my job." Although she hated her newest assignment.

"And you are good at it. Good for my son. This pleases me." The queen reached out and squeezed Grace's hand where it rested on the table.

Amir looked up from his discussion with his father, his brows drawn together in a questioning frown. "What are you two plotting?"

Assuming he was concerned she was telling his mother about his search for a wife, Grace was quick to put his worries to rest. "We were merely discussing how much you love being here."

"Grace is saddened by the fact you cannot live here full-time," the queen added.

Amir looked startled. "You should not be saddened by it. You know I do well in New York."

"Yes, of course, but you would prefer to live here."

"I could not handle my family's foreign business concerns so easily from here."

Grace did not agree, but she was unsure how to voice her argument in the current company.

Before she could find the right words, the king spoke.

"It is the way life must be," he said with a

finality that spoke volumes about his youngest son's future.

And for no reason she could fathom, Grace felt pain on Amir's behalf. After all, he *was* happy in New York, but his birthright dictated so much about his life. It was no wonder he wanted some say over the woman he ended up married to. Yet, the truth was even that was being dictated by the life he had been born into. Despite her own father's authority within their family, none of her brothers could or would be forced to marry before they were ready. For that matter, neither would she nor her sisters.

But Amir knew he was living on borrowed time in terms of choosing his own wife. The knowledge that he was as trapped in his course as Grace felt by it sent a wave of desolation, followed by pain-filled compassion, over her. She would do everything she could to make sure his life was as happy as it could be within circumstances that could not be changed.

"This begs the question what you were worried Grace was telling me," Queen Adara said, proving she knew her youngest son only too well.

"Was the report Grace compiled for you on the shipping agreement sufficient,

Father?" Amir simply shrugged and changed the subject. He might be a youngest son, but he was by no means an easily cowed man. Even when it came to his royal mother.

"Yes." The king gave Grace one of his rare smiles in approval. "You understand both our business and our country well, Miss Brown."

"I would think that after five years, you could call her Grace," Amir said, mocking humor lacing his voice. He definitely wasn't totally willing to have his life and responses dictated by his role in life.

Shocking Grace, his father inclined his head in acknowledgment. "Grace."

"Thank you, Your Majesty."

"You may call me King."

Grace almost laughed out loud, but managed to stifle the urge in time. She knew King Faruq was perfectly serious and that he believed he was bestowing a special privilege on her. Which he was. After all, the only people allowed to shorten the title were his close friends and advisors and even most of them called him My King.

"It would be an honor, King."

Grace was not surprised when the queen made no similar gesture. Early in their acquaintance, she had invited her son's assistant to use her first name when they were in private. Grace had always considered the older woman more a friend than simply the royal parent of her boss.

Grace spent that night poring over the information she had compiled on possible candidates for Amir's wife hunt. Her dedication to the project had been renewed, if without improvement to her enjoyment of it. And, in her mind, that would take a miracle of the parting-of-the-sea variety. Still, she was determined to use their time in Zorha to finish compiling the list so he could begin his campaign when they returned to New York.

She was listening to the ballads on her iPod and totally focused on the Internet research she was doing when a hand fell on her shoulder.

She jumped and screamed, falling off of her chair and yanking the bud speakers out of her ears.

She looked up from her perch on the floor, a sharp pain in her hip telling her tomorrow there would be a bruise. "Amir! What are you doing here?"

Her heart was still beating madly and identifying her surprise visitor had not improved the matter at all.

He dropped to squat beside her, his hands roving over her body, no doubt to check for damage. "Are you all right, Grace? I did not mean to scare you like that."

"I didn't hear you come in" was all she could get past a throat constricted with instantaneous desire. Having him so close was bad enough, but her body was interpreting his impersonal touches as something much more.

"That is obvious." His probing had reached the rapidly forming bruise.

She winced and let out a slight gasp of pain.

"You *are* hurt," he said accusingly.

"It's nothing major, just a bruise." She needed to move away from him, but her body had stopped listening to her mind's dictates—where he was concerned—a long time ago.

"Let me see."

Bare her lower body to him? She didn't think so. "No."

"This is no time for your stubbornness, Grace."

"I'm not taking off my clothes so you can inspect the damage and fulfill some centuries-old responsibility factor your family has toward employees."

"It is nothing I have not seen before. You can keep your panties on."

"You are not my doctor and he is the only one who sees me like that."

"I wondered," Amir said, apropos of nothing. Then he stood, lifting her to her feet as well. "If you insist on a doctor, then you shall see a doctor."

"You can't be serious! I fell off my chair, not a second-floor balcony. I'll be fine."

Something passed over his face at her mention of the balcony, but was quickly gone. "Nevertheless, we shall have you tended to."

"No." She put her hands on her hips and gave him her fiercest *I mean business* frown. "Absolutely not."

Patently unaffected, he said, "Yes. I must insist."

"Are you planning to carry me resisting all the way, because that is the only way I'm going to see a doctor for something so minor."

Amir didn't say a word, he just lifted her in his arms and started toward the door.

She screeched and pounded on his shoulder. "All right, you win!"

"You will go to the doctor under your own power?"

"No. You can inspect the bruise for yourself."

"And if I think it needs a doctor's attention?"

"I will bean you," she said unrepentantly.

"Resorting to threats of violence is no way to win a negotiation."

CHAPTER FIVE

"I AM NOT THE BULLY HERE."

"I am no bully!" He looked so totally offended and *hurt* that she had to sigh.

"No, you're not a bully, but you are irritating."

"Thank you so much," he said sarcastically.

"You can put me down now."

He did so, her brain trying to convince her it was with reluctance.

She stepped away, needing physical distance, but it did not help. Her body positively hummed with sexual energy from their close contact.

"So, let me see."

Knowing it was a bad idea, she complied, slipping her sleep shirt up high enough to reveal the purpling bruise on her hip. He reached out and brushed it oh so lightly. She shuddered and had to bite back a moan of wholly inappropriate pleasure.

"Is it that sensitive?"

"I'm just not used to being touched there." The honesty might be awkward but it was better than having him decide she needed to see a doctor after all.

Now *that* would be mortifying.

"It does not look as if any serious damage was done."

She dropped her oversized Red Sox jersey back into place. "I told you."

His thumb brushed over the spot one more time before he pulled his hand away.

It was all she could do not to demand he put it back and touch her far more intimately.

Doing her best to collect herself, she turned to face him. "You never told me why you are here."

"I saw that your light was still on."

"So? You decided to drop in and visit? Even when I didn't answer the door?"

"It is past midnight, Grace. I was concerned you had fallen asleep with the light on. I did not wish it to disturb your rest."

"So, instead, you scared me into falling off my chair."

"That was unintentional."

"No doubt. Well, now that you've seen I *did not* fall asleep with the light on, you can continue on to whatever you were doing."

"Not just yet."

"Was there something you needed to discuss?"

"Why are you still up? You have not been getting enough sleep as it is."

"You know I never sleep well the first night after a transatlantic flight."

"That was only true when we used to make the flights during the day. Once I adjusted the schedule so we could fly at night and you could sleep on the plane, it improved. Or so you said." His expression said he now doubted the veracity of her claims.

"It did. Does. I got to working…I wasn't tired." But an inescapable yawn belied her words.

Amir frowned. "You most certainly are tired. Why are you up?"

"What about you?" Changing the subject had worked in the past, but not always. "What are *you* doing up and about that you saw my light?"

"I could not sleep. I decided to go for a walk."

Her gaze flicked to her open balcony doors, through which she could see a star-filled night. "It's beautiful out there. I don't blame you."

"Would you like to accompany me?"

She wanted to, more than almost anything. But she couldn't. "Actually, I'm working," she admitted.

"On what?"

She couldn't believe he didn't guess, that he was going to make her say it. "My new project."

Recognition dawned, quickly followed by a glare of disapproval. "I told you that if it was too much, you were not to do it."

Yeah, right. "It isn't too much."

"Then why are you working at midnight when you so clearly should be sleeping?"

"Because I *want* to." She couldn't say she was in the mood to do the project, because that would never be the case. But she did want to finish it successfully for him.

"This is not acceptable. You need your rest. You will shut down your computer. I insist."

"If I go to bed right now, I won't sleep. My mind is filled with information it is sorting through." She knew he understood this.

It was a trait they shared and had often led to midnight snacks together and chats because of it. The fact that they were in the office together so late often enough to make a trip to the all-night diner nearby commonplace indicated that perhaps they were both a little too involved with their work. Only for her, it was also the desire to spend time with him, no matter what guise that time came under.

"Then you will come for a walk with me. No more working."

"You said you wanted the list today."

"Correction, I asked if you had finished it. I did not give you a deadline for completion."

"But we both know that I need to do so soon or there is a risk your father will step in again with another choice of his own."

"I will take that risk, but your health will not be compromised."

He reached toward her computer. "Is there anything you need to save?"

"No."

He nodded and then clicked on the standby key before pushing her laptop closed. "Let's go."

She looked down at her pajamas. "I need to put something on, or I will shock your guards."

"More like instigate their lust."

She laughed as she was sure his comment was meant as a joke. Though the tease hurt, she wouldn't let him see that. As she'd promised him, she was wearing her new Red Sox jersey as a nightgown. It reached her midthigh, and she sincerely doubted a glimpse at her pale, gangly legs below the hem would inspire so much as passing notice, much less lust. Certainly not in the men who guarded the palace night and day, on top of the ultra high-tech security system his father had installed three years ago. She wasn't exactly center-fold material and they were trained to keep their focus wholly on their work.

She grabbed a pair of leggings and took them into the bathroom to don them. She came out a minute later and grabbed a pair of socks from the dresser a servant had unpacked her clothing into earlier.

Amir made a choking noise. "You think that is an improvement?"

She looked up from pulling on her socks and met his dark gaze. "What is the matter? Do you think my clothes will offend?"

"I think that if you plan to leave this room, you will put something far less revealing on."

"I'm not going to get completely dressed in a business suit, hose and dress shoes, Amir."

"I do not expect you to."

"Then what is your problem?"

"Those pants might as well be painted on."

"They're leggings. I wear them to work out."

"You wear them in public back in New York?"

"If you mean, do I wear them at the gym? Then, yes. Why is this a problem for you?"

"Because they are too damn revealing."

"What difference does it make? All they reveal is how skinny my legs are."

He shook his head. "You are serious, aren't you?"

"Amir…this is getting tedious. Am I going on the walk with you, or not?"

He didn't answer. Instead, he went over to her dresser and started opening drawers. He made a noise of approval and pulled out a pair of loose, wide-legged sweatpants and a matching jacket. "These will do."

"You expect me to change?"

"Yes."

"You know I think you are being ridiculous about this, don't you?"

He simply held the clothes out to her. Considering how intransigent he had been about the doctor, she should not be surprised. Sometimes, Amir got in these stubborn moods and her only choice was to give in or table the discussion for a later time when hopefully, he would be more reasonable. Right now, it was give in, or not go.

As often happened, her need to be with him took precedence, besides maybe the leggings *would* be considered inappropriate attire for a prince's companion here in Zorha.

She rolled her eyes to show she still thought he was being silly and went to grab a T-shirt to go with the sweats. Her nightshirt would look totally dumb hanging so far below the jacket.

Once she was dressed in what Amir apparently considered appropriate attire, they left her room. He led her down to the first level and out through the door near the kitchens, which opened onto the desert surrounding the palace rather than the courtyard in the center of the compound.

Grace did not worry about getting lost. Amir knew the desert as well as she knew her own tiny apartment's layout back in New York. He led her in the direction of a nearby oasis. Or at least, she thought he did. She was going on memories from other walks and horseback rides with him on previous trips, all of which had occurred during the day.

Amir took a deep breath. "I love the smell of the desert."

All she could discern was the dry fragrance of sand. She was sure he was noticing a lot more.

"I'm sorry you miss this so much when you are in New York."

"So you said at dinner."

"You *were* listening."

"No, I asked my mother later for a more complete account of the conversation."

"Why? Didn't you trust me not to tell her about your wife hunt?" She'd thought that was his worry at dinner, but the fact he had not believed her subtle assurance to the contrary rankled. More than that, it hurt. She would trust *him* with her life.

But not knowledge of your love, a small voice said inside her brain and it sounded suspiciously like her father's tone when he chided her for her shyness.

It would only cause stress between us. He doesn't want my love, she argued back.

Are you sure about that? the voice asked.

Yes! She wished she wasn't.

"Of course," Amir said, interrupting her argument with herself. "Grace, you would never betray my confidence."

"I'm glad you realize that."

"I wanted to know what had prompted your comments."

"Did you figure it out?"

"Not really, no."

"You are my friend, Amir. I want you to be happy." For her, it was that simple. Even if she had not loved him.

"I *am* happy, Grace."

"You would be happier living here."

"No, I would not."

When she would have argued, he laid his hand on her shoulder to silence her and then left it there as they walked and he explained. "I do miss the desert when I am away from it. I miss my people, my family…all of it. But, Grace, when we are here, I also miss New York. I prefer the faster pace of life in the city on a regular basis, though I admit it is a relief to retreat here occasionally."

"You couldn't dally with your women here," she said in sudden, unpleasant understanding.

Amir laughed. "What an old-fashioned term."

"Perhaps I'm an old-fashioned girl."

"You are a treasure, dear friend."

Warmth spread through her, dispelling the coldness of her realization. "Thank you."

"According to you, I am no longer allowed to dally anyway."

She chuckled at that. "I am not your father, I cannot order you to comply with my wishes."

Amir stopped, the full moon lighting the night sky almost as bright as day and casting his face in its cool glow. "You have more daily influence on me than any other person, Grace."

"I wouldn't put it that way."

"Perhaps I should not, either," he said with an amused smile. "You will begin to think you can boss me around."

That made her laugh. "Don't worry, Amir…I will never make the mistake of believing *anyone* could boss you around."

"My father?"

"Even him. You acquiesce to his commands because you choose to do so. If he ever demanded something you could not accept, you are strong enough to walk away from your family rather than to comply."

"Like Princess Lina did."

"Do you think her family disowned her? They certainly haven't publicly and the press release about her wedding had a picture with her aunt and uncle with her and her new husband the day after they were married."

For a moment, Amir looked sad. "Her father is more dictatorial than my own. I think it is a distinct possibility."

Grace had met the princess's older brother at a function at the palace once, though not the younger sister. "I don't see her brother turning his back on her."

"Perhaps, but I guarantee my brothers would follow my father."

"I think you are wrong." The princes were fiercely loyal to one another. Even if Zahir had brought the news of their father's edict to Amir.

"It is a moot point as I have no intention of being placed in a position where I have to defy my king."

"I know. I don't know if I said, but I think you are smart to preempt his next move as you are doing." No matter how much it hurt her.

"I take your good opinion for granted," he said rather arrogantly. "It is not as if you do not tell me when you think I am doing something stupid."

This was true. She smiled. "You're right."

He shook his head again, a pained expression on his face. "You have no idea what you are doing, do you?"

"I'm standing in the moonlight with my best friend."

"Am I your best friend, Grace?"

"How can you doubt it? I have almost no time for other friendships."

Now guilt painted his features. "Perhaps we should adjust your working hours when we return to New York."

She shrugged, though pain lanced through her again. Just like on the plane, she saw this as further proof that he was pulling away from her, from their friendship. He didn't *want* to be her best friend.

"Are we going to the oasis?" she asked.

Looking around them with longing in his dark eyes, he sighed. "Actually, I think we should get back to the palace and into our beds."

"I'm sorry."

"For what?"

"I know you planned a longer walk than

this, but you are insisting on returning because you are taking care of me." And once again, she knew it would do no good to argue.

"We can both use some sleep."

But he still would not have returned so soon without her. And while that did make her feel genuinely bad, she also stored away the sensation of being cared for so kindly. If she was right and her future with him would be markedly different than her past, she would need as many warming memories as she could accumulate to take her through the colder times to come.

Amir walked into Grace's room without invitation for the second time in less than eight hours. Though he had knocked just as he had the night before. Just as then, there had been no answer. Last night she'd been listening to her music and had not heard him. He discovered that this morning, she was still sleeping. Deeply enough that she had not woken to his firm knock.

He stopped beside her bed and shook his head. She looked so peaceful, which only brought home how stressed she had been lately. She'd hidden it well, but even in her sleep on the plane she had not relaxed enough for him to see the difference. Being in Zorha was good for *her* as well.

It was almost seven and he was sure her alarm was set to go off then. He picked up the travel clock, incongruous to the décor that would have done an ancient harem proud. He didn't know what his mother had been thinking when she had assigned Grace to this bedroom. However, she was never given a different one, no matter when they came to visit or how many guests the palace was holding. He had never requested his mother change the arrangements because Grace had been overtly charmed by her accommodations and Amir liked to see his invaluable assistant happy.

Shrugging off his mother's idiosyncrasies and Grace's unexpected reaction, he flicked through the options on the small digital clock until he had turned off the alarm.

He quietly put it back on the side table. Clearly, Grace needed more sleep. If she would not listen to him, he would take matters into his own hands. The very fact that she had not woken to his knock or his presence testified to that truth. The bruises of exhaustion under her eyes actually looked better than they had yesterday and he was determined they would disappear entirely. He walked across the room and pulled the heavy drapes over the exit to the balcony, shrouding the room in a false dusk.

A day of rest would not go amiss, either. With that thought in mind, he unplugged her laptop and carried it from the room, closing the door silently behind him.

He found his mother and asked her to convey his plans for the day to Grace when she woke. He also told the queen that he wanted his assistant to spend the day relaxing. His mother assured him she would see to it.

Feeling as if he had taken care of the things in his world that needed tending, he left the palace with his father and brother.

Grace slowly surfaced to consciousness, a sensation of well-being pervading her. She'd had the most luscious dream about Amir. They had been married and deliriously in love. They were on one of their frequent trips to Zorha along with their four children. A little boy, so very serious and very much like his father at the age of ten. An eight-year-old girl who shared her grandmother's royal bearing and propensity to involve herself in the affairs of others. A sturdy little blond boy who at five years old reminded Grace of her second oldest brother and a sweet little baby girl that had surprised both her parents with her advent into the world. A very good surprise though.

The dream had been so real that Grace smiled as she stretched between the silky smooth Egyptian cotton sheets. Refusing to open her eyes, she wallowed in the joy left over from her dream. Four children? A soft laugh erupted from her throat. She could so see Amir as a doting father of a gaggle of children.

The unbidden thought that no matter how real the dream seemed *she* would *not* be their mother shattered the happiness burbling through her and Grace's eyes snapped open. The first thing she noticed was that her drapes were drawn. She didn't remember closing them last night. The second thing was that it was almost eleven o'clock. Her alarm had not gone off to wake her. She knew she had set it. She always set it. Always. The next thing she noted was that her computer was not sitting on the antique baroque desk she liked to work on when she was here in Zorha.

She sat up, the covers falling away from her as she tried to make sense of the inconsistencies. She rubbed the sleep from her eyes, but the scene did not change.

How had she slept so late? Even without the alarm, it was not normal for her. Okay, so maybe she *did* need to catch up on her sleep like Amir kept saying, not that she'd admit it to him. The man was already so sure he was always right. Of course, he would know the truth since she had just woken up and the morning was practically over.

But even if he *had* been right, that didn't explain the closed drapes, her alarm that had not gone off, or the missing computer. She had a feeling she wouldn't figure those things out until she tracked down her boss, which meant she had to get up.

Thirty minutes later, freshly showered and dressed comfortably, if not stylishly—she didn't *do* stylish—she made her way to the first floor of the palace. She was directed by one of the guards to the queen's personal study. A regal voice bade her enter when she knocked.

The queen dismissed her own assistant

when Grace came into the beautiful, feminine room that nevertheless was obviously a working office. "Good day, Grace. I trust you slept well."

"Better than I should have," Grace replied ruefully. "I slept through my alarm."

"I believe my son turned it off when he went to see you this morning."

"He came to see me?" Again?

The queen nodded. "To tell you that he would be spending the day with his father and Zahir."

"But he came into my room? Turned off my alarm?" She was going to have to talk to Amir about just barging in. She didn't make it a habit of dressing or changing in the en suite and while it probably wouldn't bother him to catch her half-naked, it would certainly upset her. "Why didn't he wake me?"

"I believe he thought you needed additional rest." The queen smiled. "He said something about confiscating your computer for the day as well."

"I've still got my handheld computer," Grace said defiantly. She had notes from her projects on it and Internet access. It wasn't as easy to use as her laptop, but it could be done.

She did not like having her activities dictated to her. Especially when it was already so hard to make herself work on her current, most pressing project.

"I had hoped you would do me the favor of giving me your company this afternoon."

Grace's heart sank. She knew without doubt that Amir was behind the queen's invitation, but that didn't make it any easier to turn it down. In fact, she couldn't think of a single way to do so without offending the monarch. "Of course, Your Majesty."

The slight elevation of the other woman's pencil-thin brow said she noticed Grace's use of her formal title despite the fact there was no one else in the room with them. But she did not call her on it.

"What did you have in mind?" Grace asked.

"I would like to do some shopping."

Grace couldn't help it. She laughed out loud.

The queen gave her a quizzical look. "What is so amusing?"

"Your son."

That seemed to startle the other woman. "My son?"

"Yes. He thought he had me all sewn up."

"Sewn up? Like a garment?"

"Sort of. He thinks he has me outmaneuvered."

"But you do not agree?"

"We are going shopping?"

"Yes."

"Then no, I do not agree."

"Do you mind explaining?"

"I assume my boss asked you to make sure I did not work today, right?"

"That is correct."

"Has he ever been shopping with you, Adara?"

The older woman was smiling herself, now. "No. He has not had the pleasure."

"I haven't for at least a year, either, but I'm looking forward to it. Let me get my purse."

"You have no need."

"Of course I do." Though she knew it would take quick action and forethought on her part to pay for any of her own purchases.

Grace smiled all the way to her room anyway. If it had been Amir's intention to make sure she relaxed today by stealing her computer, he had miscalculated badly. Shopping with his mother might be fun, but it was nowhere near restful.

CHAPTER SIX

LATER THAT EVENING, Grace relaxed in a hot bath fragrant with a special oil Adara had insisted on gifting her. Soft flower petals floated on the surface of the steaming water and brushed against Grace's skin erotically. She was sure that had not been her royal friend's intent when she had sent, via a servant, a basket filled with the floral offering for Grace's upcoming bath. The other woman had simply wanted Grace to enjoy being spoiled by the decadence. Adara was extremely kind and always had been, treating Grace with gentle courtesy not usually extended to a personal assistant by someone in the queen's position.

Grace wasn't sure, but she thought the queen might have recognized Grace's love for her son early on. She never said anything, but she had looked at the younger woman with feminine sympathy more than once.

Grace had to admit that though shopping with the queen might not be restful, it *was* relaxing. She'd managed to forget her special project entirely for big chunks of time.

"Do you ever answer your d—" Amir's voice cut off abruptly as he stood in the entrance to her private en suite bathroom.

At six foot four inches, he filled the doorway with his body. Her mind screamed that she should have had that talk with Amir over the cell phone if necessary as she gasped and sat straight up. Frantically looking for something to cover herself, she saw that the bath sheet was out of reach and the washcloth would hardly be adequate. With no other option open to her, Grace curled her knees up, hiding her nudity behind her folded legs. *"What are you doing in here?"*

"I came to speak to you." Amir's words came out disjointed and he made no move to turn away.

"Now is not a good time." She vacillated between wanting to hyperventilate and wishing the situation was something different than what it was. And no amount of inner castigation could make that desire disappear.

Amir cleared his throat. "I see that."

He definitely saw *something*. His eyes devoured her, or at least that's what it felt like. He wasn't really doing it…not to her. She wasn't his type. Not drop-dead gorgeous. Not sexually sophisticated. Not anything he usually found attractive.

The thought made her angry. "You could have knocked."

"I did knock. You did not answer."

"I didn't hear you."

"So, I came inside."

"You shouldn't have."

"You should have closed this door," he countered, again making no move to leave.

Clearly, he was so unfazed by her nudity, he planned to have whatever discussion he originally planned on. She was not so sanguine.

"I am in the private bath attached to my own bedroom, I did not think it was necessary," she said angrily.

"Apparently, you were wrong."

"Apparently, *you* forgot your manners, or is it only me you don't deem worthy of them?"

"What? Grace, you don't mean that." He looked upset, darn it.

How could he be so dense? "You need to leave, Amir."

"Leave?"

"Leave." She let out a tight breath. "I'm naked, in case you haven't noticed."

"I noticed." His voice sent shivers through her.

"Good."

"I'm not sure it is."

Frustration bubbled up inside her. "Amir, you cannot just walk into my room."

"There was no problem last night, or this morning."

So *he* said. "I want my computer back and there is definitely a problem now."

She couldn't believe they were having this discussion. Why hadn't he left the moment he realized she was in the bath? Was it because *her* nudity was so unremarkable, it didn't matter to him? She'd always know he didn't want her the way a man wants a woman, but to have him dismiss her femininity entirely was beyond demoralizing.

"I will leave."

She rolled her eyes. Finally! When had her brilliant boss ever sounded so simpleminded?

But he still didn't move.

"Amir," she said impatiently. It would be one

thing if all she felt was embarrassment, but it wasn't. Being naked in his presence brought out feelings she could not act on, but if he didn't leave she just might try. And that would be bad. Really, very, beyond normally, survivable boundaries, bad. "You need to go. *Now.*"

He seemed to shake himself. "Of course. I apologize for invading your bath."

If only he would invade her bath, and not merely her privacy.

When she said nothing in reply, he sighed deeply and then he spun on his heel, bumping into the doorway with totally unfamiliar clumsiness, and then disappearing into the room beyond.

Grace stared at the open doorway for several seconds, waiting to hear the sound of her door closing in the outer room, but the sound never came.

"Amir?" she called out. If he'd left her door open, she was going to kill him.

"I'm here, Grace." His voice sounded strained.

"I'm taking a bath. Whatever you need to discuss is going to have to wait," she said in case he had the insane idea she was going to get out of her well-earned bath and prance out there with nothing but an oversized towel wrapped around her body, only to reenact another version of the mortifying scene.

"I am aware you are taking a bath." He said something else, but she could not hear him.

"Then why are you still in my room?"

Again he muttered something that she could not make out.

She stretched her legs out in front of her, settling back into the water and trying to come to terms with the weirdness of the situation. She forced her body to relax in a further attempt to let go of the hurt lingering from his unwitting rejection.

Amir stood in Grace's bedroom, willing himself not to go back into the tiled bathroom. However, the image of Grace's pink-and-white body floating in a pool of petal-strewn water in the big Roman-style bath was burned into his brain and wreaking havoc with his logical mind.

The sound of her moving in the water nearly undid him.

Was she washing herself? Rubbing skin that looked softer than the flower petals floating around her with soap that would leave her smelling more alluring than any personal assistant ever should? Especially one as efficient and controlled and damn it…*innocent*…as Grace.

"Please stop doing that," he said in a voice that almost cracked. How he managed to control it, he did not know.

"Doing what?" she asked, sounding genuinely perplexed.

She had no idea. Innocent. Too innocent for his thoughts or libido.

"Moving, making the water splash around you."

A slow beat of silence met his words and then she asked, "Did you get too much sun today?"

He wished he had that excuse. "No," he groaned.

"I think maybe you did." He could hear her standing up in the bath. "I think maybe you need to see a doctor."

She was going to get out of the bath to check on him. If she walked out wearing nothing but a bath sheet, he was going to lose what remained of his control. His body ached for just such an eventuality, but his mind refused to be so weak.

* * *

The sound of quickly moving footsteps and a slamming door was the only answer Grace got to her suggestion about the doctor. She frowned. Deciding this situation required further action, she grabbed a towel and wrapped it around her to patter—dripping— into her bedroom. She picked up the phone and called the extension for the king and queen's suite.

The phone was picked up by the king himself. "Amir?"

"It's Grace, Your Majesty."

"King."

"King." Sheesh, right now, how she addressed him was *not* at the top of her priority list.

"I thought Amir was coming up to speak to you."

"He was here, acting strangely. Did he get too much sun today, sir?"

"Not that I'm aware of. We only spent a couple of hours riding, the rest was spent conducting business indoors."

"Perhaps the sun was especially hot?"

"I did not notice it."

"Hmm…maybe he just needs a good night's sleep."

"In what way was he acting strangely?" the king asked, sounding amused.

"He wasn't his usual brilliant self." Which was as far as she was willing to go with the explanations. No way did King Faruq need to know his son had caught her naked in the bath.

"I see." But he did not sound like he did and she wasn't about to enlighten him.

"Thank you for your time, King."

"You are welcome. You are always free to call if you have a need."

There seemed to be a message there that Grace did not get, but she simply thanked him and hung up.

She walked slowly back to the bath, her thoughts centered with concern on Amir. What had caused him to behave so out of character? And why had he come to see her in the first place? Before he had started to pull away, she would have thought he had simply wanted to tell her about his day. For the past five years, when they were apart unexpectedly, when they reconnected, they shared each of their individual experiences.

She'd heard more about his women than she wanted, but she had still enjoyed the intimacy of it.

Yet, that was no doubt *not* what he had

wanted tonight. Perhaps a business issue had come up he had wanted her input on or simply to appraise her of. Regardless, as she had told him, it would have to wait.

She climbed back into the hot water and shrugged away the worries. She could not do anything about his odd behavior, much less understand it. She might as well finish enjoying the luxury of a hopefully now *un-interrupted* bath.

Amir brought the *gumia* down in a sweeping arc, part of a thousand-year-old pattern the men in his family had learned generation after generation. The perfectly balanced, curved sword fit his hand as if it had been made for it. Which, in fact, it had.

However, as satisfying as the sword practice was in a general sense, it was not doing what he most needed at the moment— helping him to forget his reaction to Grace's naked body. It made no sense. He could accept that he was attracted to his assistant, after all sexual desire did not follow rhyme or reason. But he found it intolerable that he had been so paralyzed by the sight of her lying in the bath that he had been unable to leave the room immediately.

He had made a complete prat of himself and she had asked him if he'd gotten too much sun. He almost missed a step as he shook his head in amazement. Absolutely clueless to her own appeal.

"Would you like a practice partner?" Zahir's voice interrupted Amir's troubled musings.

He turned to face his brother, who—like him—was dressed in a pair of loose-fitting pants and nothing else. Obviously, he wanted to work out as well.

"Definitely."

Without any further discussion, Zahir brought his own sword up into the beginning stance. They sparred for thirty minutes, both of them working up a sweat as they fought for dominance. But though his brother topped him by an inch and seven years of life, Amir refused to yield the field. With silent understanding, they both dropped their *gumias* at the same time and bowed their heads to one another in acknowledgment of the other's prowess.

"Did you work out your demons?" Zahir asked.

"Why do you think I was doing that?"

"I recognize the expression in your eyes because I've seen it in my own."

Amir's own worries went to the back of his mind immediately. "Anything you wish to talk about?"

Zahir shook his head, but because Amir was looking he saw the flicker of unhappiness quickly hidden.

"Is everything all right between you and our father?" Amir probed.

His brother shrugged. "As all right as it can be between two headstrong men bent on getting their own way."

"Does he pull the sovereign card on you often?"

"No, he respects me too much for that, but…" Zahir let his words trail off with another shrug.

"I do not envy you."

Zahir dried his face, chest and arms with a small towel. "I know. You and Khalil are too smart for that kind of stuff."

"We love you," Amir said, wiping away his own sweat.

Zahir almost smiled. "I love you both as well."

"Even when you have to travel half a world away to give a message of disappointment from our father?"

A look of understanding flashed across Zahir's features. "Maybe especially then. I felt badly for you and I cannot say I regret that Princess Lina refused to submit to the contract between our fathers."

"Thank you." Maybe Grace had been right. Given the correct set of circumstances, his brothers might actually support him if he chose a path divergent from their father's wishes. Then again relief was not the same thing as righteous indignation on his behalf. "A man wants to choose his own wife."

"Yes."

"What about you? Any plans to set up a royal nursery?"

"I would need a wife first."

"And?"

"There is no one." But something about how he said it made Amir know there was a story here even if his brother was clearly not ready to share it.

"I want Grace." Amir could not believe he had said the words aloud.

But his brother did not look shocked. "Naturally, you have done nothing about it."

"She is in my employ."

"Under your protection." Grace might not understand that concept but his brother did.

"Exactly."

"Not marriage material?"

The question shocked Amir into stillness. "She is hardly a princess."

"And you are not heir to the throne—that does come with some benefits. The expectations concerning your spouse are one of them."

"I don't think our father has made it that far into the twenty-first century."

"Before Khalil married Jade, I would have said the same."

"Khalil loves Jade. He would have married her with or without our father's approval."

"And yet he humbled himself to get it."

"*Love.*" Amir was fully aware he made the single word sound like a curse—because to him, it was.

"*Inshallah.*"

As God wills it. "I suppose, but I do not want a wife that makes me that vulnerable."

"That is understandable." More than anyone, Zahir had seen what losing Yasmine had done to his youngest brother. "But it does not answer the question of Grace."

"I want her. I cannot have her. Something must be done."

"Not marriage?"

"Absolutely not."

"So, what will you do?"

"I have a plan."

"I hope it is a good one." This time the smile was complete. "You have not given me such a good workout in memory."

He hoped so, too. Because his over-the-top reaction to the relatively tame circumstance of seeing Grace naked was not acceptable. He could not make love to her. Even if he didn't feel what she called his "ancestor instincts" to protect one of his own, there was the certainty that an affair between them would result in the loss of his perfect PA.

But there was another reason, one he was only now coming to admit to himself. It was the reason marriage to Grace was not an option. He already…cared for her. Even in his own thoughts, he was reluctant to admit that. If he married her, the friendship and lust he felt toward her might become something more. It might well become the one thing he did not want.

Of all the women in the world, Grace was the one who could never be his convenient wife.

Despite having no more concrete answers to his Grace problem, Amir felt better returning to his room ten minutes later. Whoever said it was lonely at the top, knew what he was talking about.

Look at Zahir. Clearly something was bothering the heir to the throne of Zorha, but who did he have to discuss it with? Amir would have to look for an opportunity to talk with his brother again, to see if there was anything he could do for him.

Amir was glad he had his brothers and part of him wished he could see them more frequently. Another more logical part recognized that to do so would test the boundaries of all their patience and perhaps even their love. They were too alike.

Grace spent the next few days attending meetings with Amir and his family or Zorhan business associates. In between working with him, she continued pulling together his list of potential wife candidates and developing a plan of attack for securing his choice.

It went slower than she would have liked because the queen also demanded some of Grace's time each day. She certainly didn't begrudge that time. She understood how the queen missed the company of her own daughters. And Grace enjoyed the older woman's company very much, but she needed to finish the personal project for Amir.

However, the closer she got to completion, the more certain she became of a painful fact. She could not continue to work for him. The emotional distress caused by her unrequited love grew by the day now. It had to be the result of his plan to marry. Compiling the list of names *hurt*. It hurt way more than she had been prepared for and she hadn't thought it was going to be easy. But it was mental torture of the worst kind. First, creating a profile of the ideal candidate—defining the type of woman she thought the man she loved would be most happy with had shredded an already battered heart. Every requirement she listed that was something she did not possess—such as physical beauty, the right breeding and/or sophistication—made her feel badly about herself. Even worse were the traits she did share with her picture of the ideal woman for Amir. As that list grew, she couldn't help wishing *she* could be the candidate. But she lacked what he wanted physically, and without it, no amount of personality and inner depth could compensate.

Especially for Amir, who had said the only compatibility he was concerned about was what they shared in bed.

Then, looking for women who actually met her requirement caused Grace no end of pain. She envied them and that made her feel evil. She could not be so petty, but she was. It destroyed her to realize each of these women had a chance at the life she craved—to be Amir's wife. Each moment spent creating dossiers on likely candidates brought home what it was going to feel like when Amir was married to another woman as well.

It was going to be hell. And Grace had come to realize that it was not a punishment she was willing to accept, or *even capable of* withstanding. She had no choice but to leave

Amir's employ and that knowledge was decimating what bit of her sense of well-being remained.

He wasn't even engaged yet and she was beyond miserable.

The last question remaining was whether she left once she'd given him the list, or if she waited around until he actually got married. Her heart demanded she stay as long as possible, but her brain refused to ignore the way he'd pulled away from their personal relationship lately. Without his friendship, working for him would be untenable. The very heart that grieved at thoughts of her leaving would be demolished if she stayed. Watching him choose and then woo his intended would be the kind of torture she would not wish on her worst enemy—if she had one.

That thought, she had come to acknowledge, answered the question of *when* it would be best to leave. As soon as possible. Didn't they say that a clean cut hurt less than a slow, jagged incision? She certainly hoped that was true, because she didn't know how much more pain she could handle.

* * *

Amir noticed that Grace was looking more and more drawn each day, and when his mother brought it up to him, he knew he had to do something about it. He did not want Grace coming down sick.

He would take her to visit Khalil and his new wife, Jade. Grace had said before that she enjoyed their company. They had bought a new house outside the city Amir had not yet seen. And he would welcome the opportunity to ask Khalil if he knew what was going on with Zahir. There would be the added benefit of being near Athens, too. The city boasted a nightlife that could easily distract Grace from her current obsessive focus on work.

She'd always been dedicated, but the only time she wasn't on the phone, her PDA or the computer, was during mealtimes they shared with his parents or when his mother managed to pry Grace away. He knew she was working late into the night as well, though he had not made the mistake of going to her room again. But on his frequent nocturnal walks, he had noticed light beneath her door. Even if he had not noticed that, he would know she'd been staying up too late, though. Because she looked tired and was drinking entirely too much coffee.

A weekend in Athens was exactly what she needed. And he would make sure she left her work behind at the palace.

CHAPTER SEVEN

GRACE LOOKED OUT the window as Amir's family jet circled for landing at a small airport outside of Athens. No doubt Khalil would have sent a car to meet them, or the diplomat would be there himself. She'd made token protests about this trip to Amir, but her heart had not been in them. She liked the couple very much and now that she had decided to give her notice along with her report on potential wife candidates to Amir, she knew this would be her last chance to see them. Once she no longer worked for her sheikh, the lives of the Zorhan Royal Family would be off-limits to her.

Amir did his usual check of her seat belt as they came in for landing. Though technically it was the steward's job to make sure she was buckled in, she couldn't remember a single flight Amir had not seen to the matter himself. It was one of the many things she was going to miss terribly about him, but she was a grown woman. She didn't need a sheikh whose mental processes reflected those of his ancestors taking care of her like that. She didn't.

"It will be good to see Khalil again," Amir said.

"Yes. He and Jade are good people."

"Of course, they are my family."

She smiled at Amir's arrogance. "I'm sure your brother says the same about you."

"That I am good?" he asked.

"That you are good because you are related to him."

"That is not what I meant."

She laughed at his look of chagrin. "I know."

A satisfied expression came over his features. "I knew this trip was a good idea."

"It was. Thank you."

"Wait until you see what I have planned for tonight."

"Spoiling your PA or your brother and his wife?"

"You, Gracey…you have been working too hard." She loved it when he called her that, but it was really infrequent and occurred only when he was feeling more than usually protective of her or charitable toward her.

"You're a good boss, Amir."

"Naturally."

She was still laughing when the plane's landing gear made contact with the tarmac.

Khalil and Jade were both waiting in the courtesy room of the small airport that catered to the wealthy and famous. Khalil looked a lot like his brothers and Jade was as gorgeous as a model. Grace smiled at them both as the brothers embraced and kissed cheeks in greeting. Of course, Amir's greeting with Jade was less physical. Though she did insist on a hug, which made her husband frown, though he tried to hide it.

Jade laughed at his expression before turning to Grace and hugging her warmly. "He's an unreconstructed man for sure, but I love him."

Grace grinned. "It shows. And he's a lucky man."

"You're so nice, Grace. How have you handled working so closely with my reprobate brother for so many years?" Khalil asked.

"He may be autocratic on occasion and more than a little demanding with a tendency toward workaholism, but he's definitely not a reprobate."

Everyone laughed as Amir mock-glared at her. "Damned by faint praise, I believe."

"Everyone knows Grace thinks you've hung the moon," Khalil said with a one-armed hug for his younger brother.

In that moment, Grace wondered if Amir's entire family were aware of her love for him. She'd always thought it was just his mother, but the way both Khalil and Jade looked at her for the briefest moment said maybe they did, too. A month ago she would have been horribly upset that her secret was so exposed, but now it hardly mattered.

She'd always worried that Amir would discover her love for him and fire her because of it, but now that she was leaving anyway, it did not matter. That did not mean she wouldn't be embarrassed for him to learn of it, but she didn't think Khalil or Jade were the type of people to tell tales out of school.

She hoped so anyway. That was the secret she'd like intact until she told Amir goodbye.

The trip to the couple's new house took

only thirty minutes from the airport. "We like to be close to the city for both our jobs, but it is nice to live outside the congestion of Athens, especially for starting a family," Jade said as they pulled into a circular drive.

The couple shared a secretive look.

Amir grinned at his brother. "You have something to share, Khalil?"

"Not before we tell Father and Mother."

But the words were confirmation enough and Grace gave Jade an impulsive hug. "Congratulations! You're going to make a wonderful mother."

Jade beamed. "Thank you."

"She does not even suffer from morning sickness," Khalil said as if he was personally responsible for that blessing.

"My mother didn't with me, either," Jade said.

"That's fabulous." Though Grace thought that she wouldn't care if she had to suffer the pregnancy malady if it meant she could carry Amir's baby.

"It really is. I wouldn't have cared, of course, but it's nice to feel so good."

Grace nodded while Amir pounded his brother's back in congratulations.

* * *

Amir sat with Khalil on the lower terrace overlooking his brother's beautifully land-scaped gardens and swimming pool. "This is a good place to raise children."

"That is what Jade thought. So we bought it."

"You are besotted, Khalil."

"Absolutely. I cannot imagine living without her." The naked vulnerability in his brother's eyes brought back painful memories of a time when Amir had been so weakened.

He would never go there again. He could only hope for his older brother's sake that Khalil never experienced the cost such feelings could bring with them.

Grace was surprised to learn that Amir's plans for the evening did not include the newlyweds.

"You need to relax completely and as much as I love my family, spending time with them will keep you feeling as if you have to maintain a certain level of focus. I have seen it before."

"You do not think I feel the same need around you?"

"Grace, we have spent the better part of five years living practically in one another's pockets. Any worry you had about putting the right foot forward with me had to have disappeared a long time ago or you would be crazy by now."

It was true, but she was surprised he knew her so well. On the other hand, why should she be? He was right. They had spent more time together over the years than either of them had spent with anyone else. Even Amir with his women if you added them all together.

Had she made the mistake of thinking that because she had hidden her love from him, that she had hidden the rest of herself as well? If she had, she now knew better.

"Thank you. I adore your family, but this *is* nice," she said, indicating the small Mercedes coup that Amir had led her to earlier.

"It drives like a dream," he said, tongue firmly in cheek.

She laughed. "You know that the car is not what I was talking about."

"Oh, you mean this time just to ourselves? I agree. It is one of the things I miss about New York when we are over here visiting my family and conducting business."

If he missed it so much, why had he been so adept at avoiding any time alone with her in Zorha?

She asked herself if it mattered and

realized it did not. Tonight was hers. He was hers…or sort of anyway. He was her companion for the night and if her hungry heart wanted to pretend it was more for a few hours, who would it hurt? Certainly, *she* could not hurt any more than she already did.

At least, for tonight, she could lose the pain in the fantasy.

"So, where are we going?" she asked.

"You will see when we get there."

"You are such a control freak sometimes."

"Not merely a man who wishes to surprise his friend with something special?"

"Well, put that way…I'll sit back and patiently wait to arrive."

"Good woman."

When they arrived, Grace couldn't stop looking around her. As many times as they had visited Zorha, she had never watched traditional dancers. Here they were in Greece, but Amir had managed to find a Middle Eastern restaurant that provided entertainment with the multicourse meal.

She steeled herself to deal with watching Amir watch other women who were not only beautiful, but sensual, too. They performed dances that showcased not only their bodies but also the amazing amount of control they had over them. She prepared herself to see lust in Amir's expression and to have his attention on the dancers—not her—during dinner. It would not matter, she told herself. She was determined to enjoy the show as well, if for entirely different reasons.

However, the lust-filled looks never came. While Amir showed evident pleasure in her fascination with the dancers and their finely honed talents, he, himself, barely watched them. Most of his attention and all of his charm was directed at his companion…namely, her.

It was a heady feeling and she reveled in it, loving the sensation of being the focus of his concentration. They laughed at the mess they made eating with their fingers and if sometimes when they touched, her entire body jolted with the pleasure of it, she wasn't telling. The dinner was several courses and lasted late into the night with a plethora of entertainment, including men who swallowed their swords, as well as fire.

After Grace's fifth gasp, Amir laughed.

She flicked her attention from the dancer juggling fire wands. "What?"

"You are like a child at the bazaar for the first time."

"I've never seen any of this in person. I always thought they faked it somehow, but they don't, do they?"

"No."

"Isn't it amazing to you, even if you have seen it all before?"

"You make it new for me, thank you."

She felt the blush climbing her cheeks and could do nothing about it. She smiled and then looked back at the show, not sure what to say, but feeling warm and tingly all through her body.

He muttered something, but when she looked at him as if to ask what, he shook his head and took a bite of food.

They returned to Khalil and Jade's home extremely late and Grace was careful to be quiet so she would not wake them. Amir was the same, so the end to her perfect evening was a quickly whispered good-night and thanks in the hall outside their bedroom doors.

The next day, they had a leisurely breakfast with Amir's family before Khalil had to leave for a meeting. Jade stayed home to work out of the home office her husband had installed for her volunteer position with a nonprofit children's agency.

"I'll cut my hours to less than a dozen a week after the baby is born, but until then, I'll be very busy training my replacement," she said with apology for leaving Amir and Grace to their own devices for a few hours.

"Do not worry about it, Jade. I plan to take Grace sightseeing today."

Grace smiled, remembering the other times Amir had either given in to her urging to explore a new locale or had come up with the idea himself when their travels took them someplace that held interest. "Where are we going?"

"What did I tell you last night?"

"That you are an acknowledged control freak?" she teased.

He shook his head, his expression of false exasperation not quite hiding his amusement.

Jade laughed as well and went off to her office shaking her head.

They spent the day visiting tourist spots he had always resisted going to before and she felt very spoiled for a mere personal assistant. She had told Amir he was her best friend, but she knew better than to think the moniker went both ways. However, he was treating her with special consideration that if he but knew was making her final days in his employ more special than she could have conceived of. She stored up the memory of her pleasure in his company along with the others she planned to pull out in the years ahead when the only piece of him she would be able to get was what she would be able to find in the media.

They had dinner with Khalil and Jade, and Grace could not help watching the way Amir's older brother treated the woman he loved. It was incredibly sweet. He was so obviously in love, but then that emotion was patently mutual. He watched over her so carefully and even when they argued, the underlying joy they had in one another's company was always there.

It was beautiful.

And if Grace needed any more evidence that Amir had no inkling of the same feeling for her, it was there. Khalil's attention was always on Jade. Even when he was speaking to someone else, part of him was tuned in to Jade and what she was experiencing. He often called her beautiful and complimented so many things about his wife.

They did not agree on everything, not even when it came to ordering their dinner, as, apparently, Jade preferred a spicier fare than Khalil considered good for her. They compromised on something Grace got the distinct impression had been Jade's first choice to begin with. She was sure of it when the other woman winked at her while her husband was engaged with the waiter.

They all chatted and laughed over dinner until the subject of Amir's almost wedding came up.

"I was surprised the princess eloped with another man, but I was not disappointed," Khalil said.

"Why is that?" Amir asked.

"A man wants to choose his own wife."

"A woman he can love," Jade added.

Amir shook his head. "Had Father not chosen her, I would have been most content to marry the princess. I am not looking for love."

"Why not?" Jade asked in shock. "This isn't the Middle Ages, you don't have to settle for a marriage of convenience simply because you are a royal sheikh."

"Love comes with a cost I have no desire to pay."

"Yasmine's death was an unfortunate accident, my brother, but you cannot believe that any woman you chose to give your heart to would suffer a similar fate."

"There is no chance of that happening because I will not give my heart away."

Jade cast a sidelong glance of sympathy at Grace. "That's no way to live, Amir… afraid of love."

"I fear nothing. I simply refuse to travel down a path I know is rife with pitfalls."

"Well, you have time enough to change your mind now that Father's plan was subverted by the princess's flit."

Amir said nothing, but Grace knew the truth. Her boss wasn't going to wait for his father to act again and it was up to her to protect him from himself. No matter how much it hurt. And she'd done it. The list was finished, along with the plan of action for the courtship.

Amir would be impressed. Heck, Grace was impressed with herself. She almost regretted that she would not be around to see the plan put into action. Almost. It was time for the torture of her heart to stop and she was the only one who could end it.

* * *

They spent one more night in Greece and then flew back to Zorha early Monday morning. Amir and Grace had a meeting with an investment group. He had decided to give their quarterly report in person since they were available to do so. His father planned to attend the meeting as well and Grace knew that pleased Amir. He was in a good mood and she had decided to wait until after the meeting to give him her own report…and the other typed message she had printed off that morning.

Perhaps that made her a coward, but why put him in a cranky frame of mind before he had to lead an important meeting? There was plenty of time to inform him of her decision. The time after she'd done so stretched out in an unending ribbon of loneliness in her mind.

Amir waited for Grace in the office he used when he was staying in his family's home. She had said she wanted to discuss something with him. He thought she might have finished the convenient marriage proposal. There was a familiar settled air about her that she got when she was done with a difficult or involved project.

He understood her desire to present it to

him now, rather than waiting until they returned to New York. What he did not understand was his own reticence to her doing so. He'd meant what he said to his brother and Jade in Greece. Amir had no interest in falling in love and becoming vulnerable to the pain he had barely survived when he was eighteen.

Admitting how close he had come to losing everything, even to himself, was unsettling. It was difficult enough to realize that he had a measure of vulnerability when it came to his family and even Grace, but never again would he be so wrapped up in another person that losing her made him feel as if his own life were over. Khalil didn't even bother to pretend he didn't feel that way, and while part of Amir admired his brother's courage, another part pitied him his naive belief that the joy now was worth the pain later.

Grace walked into the office with only a single light tap on the door to announce her presence.

He turned away from the e-mail that had not been holding his thoughts anyway.

She looked so serious, her hazel eyes behind her glasses reflecting a level of concentration that told him his earlier supposition had been correct. And suddenly he knew that regardless of logic he did not want to deal with this right now. When they returned to New York would be soon enough.

She went to lay a plain tan binder on his desk and he had to control the urge to tell her not to.

His gaze flicked down to the modest binder and then back up to her. "The project you took on before we left New York, I presume."

"Yes. I think you will be satisfied with the results."

"I'm sure I will. Your work is always exemplary."

"Thank you."

What was that tone in her voice? An emotion he could not quite identify.

"I will look it over. We can discuss it after returning to New York."

"You do not wish for me to present it to you now?"

"No." The single word came out more vehemently than he had intended.

Her eyes widened in surprise. "Okay."

"I want to have a chance to digest the information before we talk about it."

"No problem." But she didn't look any less single-minded.

"Was there something else you wished to discuss with me?"

"Yes."

When she made no move to hand him anything else and remained oddly silent, he prompted, "What?"

She opened her mouth and only a dry croak came out.

"Are you all right?"

She nodded, cleared her throat then said, "I wanted to give you this."

Were his eyes playing tricks on him, or was her hand trembling as she dropped the single sheet of paper on the desk in front of him? Wondering what could possibly cause such a reaction in her, he picked it up. As he read it, he went first hot then cold as fury unlike anything he had ever experienced with her welled up inside him.

He surged up from his chair and tossed the paper down on the desk. "What is the meaning of this?"

"It is my letter of resignation."

"I damn well know what it is…." He slipped into Arabic curses that would have made his father blush and his mother faint. "What I want to know is what the hell it means?" he finally managed to say in English, his accent thicker than it had ever been since his tutors had begun his language studies.

Not for a millisecond did he think the letter anything but genuine. Though he wished it was a practical joke. One in very bad taste, but he knew he was not so lucky. He knew from her reaction that she intended to leave him, what he wanted to know now was *why*. It had to be something he could fix. The alternative was completely unacceptable.

"It means that I will be leaving your employment a month from today." Her tone was neutral, but the way she held her body said the control over it had been hard fought.

"Why?" he asked in a voice as close to a growl as a human male could get.

CHAPTER EIGHT

SHE BIT HER LIP, her facade cracking slightly, but she said nothing.

His fury ratcheted up another notch. Miss Efficient, the PA that always had a reason for everything, had nothing to say about leaving his employ…about leaving him? He did not damn well think so. "Is it because you got a better offer? From who? Is it Jerry? Trust me, if that is the case, he will regret attempting to take what is mine."

"I don't belong to you, Amir. I'm a personal assistant, not a slave."

Like hell she did not belong to him. "You are not leaving me."

"I am."

"I'll ruin him."

From the flare of her eyes, he knew she understood he meant what he said. "I'm not taking a job with Jerry."

Amir gave her a disdainful look.

"I'm not," she insisted.

"Then why?" He gave her no chance to go on before demanding, "Tell me it is not about money. You know I will pay you more." He would pay her pretty much anything. "If you are feeling too hemmed in in that small apartment we will find you a larger one and the company will pay for it."

"It's not about money or apartments." Her expression was pained.

What did she have to be pained about? She was the one threatening to leave him. "Then. Tell. Me. Why."

"Personal reasons."

"Personal reasons?" he asked in disbelief. Not that she had them, but that she thought she could fob him off with something so vague. "What are these *personal reasons?*"

"By definition, they are personal. That makes them not your business." The words were defiant but her tone was ragged with hurt. What was going on?

"In the past, you did not make such distinctions."

"That was in the past. This is now."

"And what has changed?"

She opened and closed her mouth without speaking, then sighed and clenched her hands at her sides. "*Me*. I'm what has changed, Amir."

"You are not so faithless."

"This isn't about loyalty. I'm not going to a competitor. I doubt I will even stay in New York. I just have to move on with my life."

"Why? Your life as my personal assistant is not a bad one."

"No, but it does not allow me to have any other life, either."

"You have never complained before."

"I'm not complaining now."

"But you *are* leaving."

"Yes."

"So, we change your hours. You get more of what you consider a life."

"It won't work, as long as I work for you, it won't work." The words sounded like they carried heavier meaning, but for the life of him he could not figure out what it was.

He was still supremely angry, but hurt was crowding in, too. "You said I was your best friend."

"But I'm not yours."

"You are leaving because you do not

think you are my best friend?" he asked with disbelief.

"Because I *know* I'm not."

"On what do you draw this conclusion?"

"On the fact that you do have a life outside your job. You have a family you see much more often than I see my own. Your siblings are your friends. You have your women and soon you will have a wife."

"And you only have me, is that what this pity party is all about?"

Anger flashed in Grace's eyes. "It's not a pity party. I'm simply trying to explain my decision to you."

"But you are leaving because I have more friends than you do," he said derisively.

"I'm leaving because I need to in order to move forward in *my* life. It's as simple as that."

"There is nothing simple about you abandoning me."

"It's not abandonment."

"You are my best friend," he admitted through gritted teeth. He hated this touchy-feely stuff, but for Grace he could make an exception.

"No, I am not."

"Damn it—"

"No, you listen. Since we came to Zorha, even before really, you've been pushing me away, pushing me into a box that is labeled *personal assistant* and nothing else. I understand it," she said, though clearly it bothered her. "You are getting married, it would not be comfortable for you to continue our friendship under those circumstances."

"That has nothing to do with it!"

"Please, you've never lied to me before, don't start now."

"How do you know I have never lied?" he demanded, his wrath at her wrong assumptions adding to the miasma of feelings inside him. "I lied every damn day when I pretended I wanted nothing more than a friendly business relationship with you, when what I wanted was to lay you across my desk and taste every centimeter of your pale skin. This is why I have pushed you away as you say. I could not risk being alone with you." And if she thought he found that easy to admit, she did not know him as well as he thought she did.

"What?" She shook her head, as if she could not translate what she had heard. "You don't mean that," she said faintly.

"I most assuredly do."

"You can't."

"And why do you believe this?"

"I'm not beautiful. I'm not sophisticated. I'm nothing like the women you usually go for."

"And yet you are the one I crave."

"No."

"Why do you attempt to deny it? You want me also."

"What? Why…I don't understand."

"What is there to understand? This desire." He stood up so she could not miss the physical evidence of his desire. "It is mutual."

She stared at him, her gaze not leaving his face. He shook his head.

"So damn innocent."

"What?"

"You."

"I'm innocent?"

"You wish to deny it?"

"Uh…no."

"It excites me, your innocence."

"But I thought you liked experienced women."

He was around his desk in a heartbeat and pulling her body into his a second heartbeat later. "I like you, Grace."

She stared up at him as if he were some alien come to earth to devour her, though she did not seem overly upset by the prospect. "You want me?" she asked with incredulity.

"I want you." Then he kissed her.

Despite his anger, regardless of the lust finally getting release, he could be nothing but gentle. It was, after all, their first kiss. And perhaps for his deceptively plain assistant, the first one she had ever had. She tasted sweet, like ripe berries, and her lips were so soft. Perfectly formed to give his mouth pleasure. She did not return the caress, but neither did she attempt to push him away.

He lifted his mouth from hers. "Kiss me back."

She looked at him with shock-glazed eyes. "I don't know how."

"Move your lips with mine, open them so I can taste you."

"Yes." The word came out sounding like a moan and he renewed the buss of his lips against hers with added passion.

She did as instructed and he was careful not to overwhelm, but to slowly lead her from innocent exploration to carnal bliss. His hands roamed up and down her back as he pressed his hardness against her, for the first time not worried that she could feel it. He wanted her to know how much she turned him on.

She made a sweet little mewling sound, her fingers kneading his chest.

His cousin Hakim sometimes called Catherine his kitten, and for the first time Amir understood such an endearment.

He tasted her mouth's interior, and the candied berries-and-cream flavor of her lips was even more luscious inside her mouth. It was a confection he could easily become addicted to.

The kiss grew in intensity and his virginal PA was learning quickly how to drive him wild. It took all of his self-control not to do what he had told her he wanted to—to strip her, lay her across his desk and use his mouth all over her.

One day, he vowed, he would do exactly that.

Suddenly, she shoved herself from his arms. "No, wait…why are you doing this?"

"What do you mean, why? I want you. I said it." Was this one of those women things that men had no hope of understanding?

"Do you? Or are you trying to use sex to manipulate me?"

Shock coursed through him. "Do you really think such a thing of me?"

"You're ruthless when negotiating."

"I have no ulterior motives." Though that plan of attack had its merits.

If she was going to leave anyway, his biggest reason for not taking her to his bed was negated. A case *could* be made that protecting her included becoming her first lover. He would make sure her introduction to sex was a pleasant one. He also would not make false promises or use her and she *did* want him.

She was frowning at him. "I won't be your mistress while you marry another woman. You promised you would be faithful, remember?"

"I did not say I wished to conduct an affair after my marriage, but you are the one who says I cannot be seen with other women at this time. Yet, there can be no issue of me being seen with you."

"So, I'm *convenient?* Any female body will do?"

What did she want from him? Was this that latent streak of romanticism showing again? "Do not analyze this to death. You are not likely to get many offers like mine. Take what I offer and make us both happy."

She didn't bother to ask what he was offering. But saying a word he never thought would pass Grace's lips, she spun on her heel and she slammed out of his office with all the drama of a woman scorned, not an innocent, *über*efficient assistant who hadn't had a real date in five years.

Amir let a curse of his own out of his mouth, then spun and threw his fist against the wall. The pain did nothing to clear his head.

What had just happened? One second he was kissing Grace. *Finally.* And enjoying it very much. The next she was spouting accusations and then storming from the room. Okay, possibly that was at least partially his fault. He had not meant his words like they had come out. But damn it, she was threatening to leave him. So, some of his anger had come out in the things he had said. And she had left.

One thing he knew—he was not going to let Grace go, easily or otherwise.

Grace stormed into her room, the desire to smash something strong. But this was not really her room and she could not afford to replace any of the objects in it, except maybe the alarm clock on the table. Without another thought, she picked up the hapless piece of electronic equipment and threw it against the wall with all her might.

The plastic shattered satisfyingly.

She looked around for something more, but saw nothing. Frustrated, she did the only thing she could think of and threw *herself* across the bed. Then the tears came and they didn't slow down. Not for a long, long time. She cried over Amir's cruel words, but she also cried over five years of unrequited love. She cried for a future without the man that she was ready to punch, but still loved beyond reason.

And she cried for the pathetic creature she knew herself to be. Amir was her whole world and she was only a tiny part of his. Sure, replacing her would be difficult, but not impossible. She was nothing but a convenient body to him. Both in the office and out of it apparently.

Memories she would rather left her alone began to surface and she knew that assessment was unfair. Amir had treated her like someone special in his life, even if she was nothing more than his PA. The knowledge only made her cry harder.

How could he say that about her not getting a lot of offers? Okay, so it was true, but did he have to rub it in? Only he had not kissed her like a man who was only scratching an itch. She could feel the restraint he had exercised. He'd made her first kiss all that it should be, even teaching her patiently with his own actions how to respond.

Then he'd ruined it with those same lips mouthing horrible words. But he'd been angry. Much angrier than even she had envisioned. And maybe a little hurt.

How much of his words were lashing out and how much truly reflected what he thought? With anyone else, she would have taken his comments at face value, but this was Amir. And she knew him better than anyone else did. Even if she wasn't his best friend. *Only he'd said she was.*

What was the truth and what was the lie?

He said he wanted her—her, Grace Brown, average-looking, gangly and unsophisticated. The way he talked, he'd wanted her for a long time. And his withdrawal hadn't been about no longer wanting her friendship. It had been the result of how difficult he found it to resist her.

Could *that* be true? She'd said he had never lied to her—and he hadn't. Which meant she should believe what he'd said. One, he did want her. Two, he had for a long time. Three, he did not want her to leave.

That one she had no trouble believing.

Her gaze fell on the copy she'd kept of the project proposal—in some masochistic favor she could not understand even now. New questions started swirling in her mind. Hope that refused to die, probably because it was linked to a love that never would, sprang in her breast.

She had believed he didn't want her, but she had been wrong. What else had she been wrong about? She thought about the makeover shows she watched sometimes when she had a rare free hour. Women who looked positively homely came out the picture of sleek sophistication. Could she do that to herself?

Was there a chance she could create the perfect candidate for Amir's marriage of convenience? His only stipulation had been that they be compatible in bed. If that kiss was anything to go by, that wasn't going to be a problem. She could read up on the subject…

this time without hiding the books away when they got to parts that made her uncomfortable. She could even watch videos…not porn, but instruction videos. Sex was a big industry, there had to be something like that out there.

Grace sat up, more resolute than she had ever felt before.

If there was any way of making her boss see her as not only a potential candidate for his wife search, but also as *the best one,* then she was going to do it.

When it came to him, hadn't she always found a way to be what he needed? The only thing she had truly lacked was the knowledge that he wanted her as a woman. He might deserve a princess…her newfound confidence faltered—maybe he really did. But no other woman, no matter how royal or beautiful or *anything*, would ever love him like Grace. Of that she was absolutely certain.

It didn't even matter if he never loved her, as long as they belonged to each other, that would be enough. It would be so much more than she thought she could have. And she wasn't stopping him from finding love elsewhere because he didn't want it. He had as much chance of finding happiness with her as anyone else.

It was her very own pot of gold at the end of the rainbow. *She'd made the rain,* she thought, as she wiped away the wetness from her cheeks.

Now it was time to travel the rainbow.

CHAPTER NINE

"YOU ARE UP EARLY, little brother."

Amir looked up from his *gumia* practice. "I am often up early."

"But not down here, working up such a sweat."

Amir considered his damp, slick skin. "In New York, I go to the gym."

"And here, we have no punching bags?"

"Precisely."

"More demons?"

"The same ones, just bigger today than before."

"Do you want to talk about it, or work at exorcising them some more?" Zahir was not dressed for sparring, but Amir had no doubts that his older brother would change if he asked him to.

His hand clenched around the handle of his curved sword as he considered his brother's offer. He'd spent forty-five minutes down here already. He felt no closer to peace—much less resolution of his quandary—than he had when he first entered this room. It had been set aside years before his birth for royal family members who were training in the old fighting ways or, more recently, wanted to work out.

He'd often come here to work out his body while he cogitated on a problem. And left feeling better for it. This morning, it had not worked.

But then, never before had he faced such a predicament.

"Talk?" he asked.

Zahir's eyes widened as if the answer surprised him, but he nodded. "Then, let us talk."

"I am not interrupting your own workout?" Obviously, his brother had come down here for something.

But Zahir shook his head. "No."

"Perhaps we could go for a ride?" It was a compromise, but only if they did not spend the entire time talking. His brother would get no workout *walking* his horse.

"I will meet you in the stables in twenty

minutes." Not only alpha, but firstborn as well and it showed.

Amir allowed himself a small smile at the other man's natural inclination to dictate terms. "Sounds good."

He was showered and in the stables fifteen minutes later.

"You are fast," his brother said as he finished inspecting the tack on the tall Arabian gelding that belonged to Amir.

His own black beast of a stallion was already saddled and waiting. They swung up onto their mounts at the same time, but Amir allowed Zahir to lead them out into the desert.

"So, what has you in such a quandary, little brother?" Zahir asked after some minutes of silent travel.

"She's leaving me."

"Grace?"

"Who else?"

"Well, you could have been talking about one of your women...Tisa perhaps."

"I told you I broke it off with her."

"You could have gotten back together. After Princess Lina eloped with her business tycoon."

"Not likely," Amir said with unconscious

derision. Tisa might be gorgeous, fun to spend time with and quite intelligent—but she wasn't the woman he wanted.

"I see. So, it is Grace we are discussing?"

"Yes."

"And she is leaving you?" Zahir frowned. "I admit, that surprises me."

"I also."

"Why is she going?"

"She cited *personal reasons*."

"And she refused to divulge what they were."

"Yes. It is very unlike her."

His brother made a sound that if Amir had not known it was out of the bounds of reality, could have been mistaken for laughter. "I see. Naturally, this upsets you."

"Yes. She is the best personal assistant I will ever have. She is perfect for me."

"And you still want her."

He averted his gaze to the surrounding desert. "Yes."

"Are you going to take her?" Zahir did not sound at all judgmental, but merely curious.

"She is a virgin."

"That is uncommon at her age, is it not?"

"Well, some commentators say that celibacy is growing in popularity in the American culture, but Grace is not merely a virgin. She is completely innocent. She does not date."

"She has no admirers?"

Amir thought of Jerry and scowled. "She has some."

"But *you* do not want to marry her?"

"No, that has not changed."

"But your determination not to have her has?"

He sighed. "You know me well."

"We are brothers."

"Yes." And he was grateful for it. "She is a romantic. It is not something I knew about her, but now that I do, I am afraid that element to her nature will leave her lonely or getting hurt."

"You were unaware of Grace's romantic nature?" Zahir asked, his voice tinged with disbelief.

"You knew of it?" Amir asked, unaccountably jealous.

"I remember well her response to our mother assigning her to the harem-style room."

"And from that, you deduced she is a romantic?"

"Yes." And the look Zahir gave Amir said he wondered why his younger brother had not.

Amir frowned, but did not have a reply to that. So, he went back to his earlier point. "Be that as it may, I now wonder if her lack of dates is the result of some romantic ideal she has created in her mind that can never be met by a flesh-and-blood man."

"You think introducing her to her sensual nature will help her overcome her obsession with this fantasy?"

"She is vulnerable to me as she is not to other men. Perhaps I can help her realize that sex is not love, which would leave her more open to other connections and she would not be so alone." Something vicious moved in his heart at the thought of Grace with some future, faceless stranger, but he ignored it. "I will not lie to her, or make promises I have no intention of keeping."

"This is how you justify taking her innocence?"

"You think I am wrong?"

"I believe you need Grace more than you are willing to admit."

"I have already admitted I will be lost without her."

"Yes."

"But?"

"Did I say anything?"

"You are thinking something."

"You want her enough to overcome your natural and very good reasons for leaving her alone. Those reasons are strongly ingrained inside you. For you to set them aside, your feelings must be very deep."

"I have not denied I want her."

"You are so sure it is only physical?"

"She is my friend, too. *My best friend.*"

His brother looked at him for several seconds of silence, broken only by the sound of the horses. Finally, he gave one of his rare smiles. "You must do what you think best, of course, but I think your plan to make love to Grace will, in the end, do her no disservice."

Amir couldn't hide his shock. He had expected his brother to take him to task for being selfish and creating arguments that were nothing less than self-serving. "Are you serious?"

"Yes, but I expect to be the best man at your wedding. After all, I am the oldest." With that, Zahir kicked his stallion into a gallop.

Amir's innate competitive streak took over and he kicked his own horse into a gallop, leaning over its neck to increase their speed. He did not know what his brother's desire to be his best man—once he'd found his convenient wife—had to do with Grace, but a certain relief lent strength to his movements as he encouraged his horse to run faster.

Zahir did not think Amir was wrong to seduce Grace. He understood Amir's arguments, which meant they were stronger than they seemed even to him.

Good. Because he did not think he could prevent himself from pursuing Grace intimately. Not after the kiss they shared. Not after she threatened to leave him.

Grace woke up feeling better than she had in two months. She had a plan and as Amir had said on more than one occasion, *Grace Brown with a plan is a fearsome thing.*

She rushed through her morning ablutions and then went straight to the queen's study. Grace was a strong proponent of going to a professional for advice. When it came to changing her image, she figured no one could give her better counsel than Queen Adara.

She was let in by the queen's assistant.

Adara looked up from a pile of papers

spread before her. They looked like calendar sheets.

"Working on your schedule?"

The older woman rubbed her temple. "Yes. It is no small feat now that my daughters are married to their own sheikhs and have separate calendars I must take into account when creating my own schedule. The travel coordination alone is enough to challenge even the most adept tactician."

Grace smiled in sympathy. "Are you using the new scheduling program I recommended last year?"

"Yes, but even with it, the events must first be discovered—" she indicated the multiple calendars strewn across the table "—then entered into the system."

"Though it has made things much easier to track," her assistant added.

"Can I do anything to help with this?" Grace asked, indicating the papers.

"Amir does not need you to work with him today?" the queen asked in surprise.

"I've decided to take a day off."

Now the queen's eyebrows climbed to her hairline. She turned to her assistant. "Will you please fetch coffee from the kitchen? I believe we are going to need it."

The young woman left and then Adara turned her attention to Grace. "Tell me what is happening."

"What do you mean?"

"You have worked for my son for five years." The queen reached out and grasped Grace's wrist.

"Uh-huh."

"Have you ever, once, in all that time, taken a day off like this?"

Grace found herself being gently, but firmly, pulled until she was seated beside Adara. "Um, no."

"So, spill…"

Grace laughed. "You don't sound much like a queen right now."

Adara did not smile. "I do not suppose I do. What I should sound like is a concerned friend and mother, for that is what I am."

"I want to change my image," Grace blurted out.

Several expressions chased across the queen's features. First shock. Then speculation. Then satisfaction. "Finally."

"Excuse me?"

"I have been hoping for more than four years for you to come to me with such a request."

"You think I look that bad?" Grace asked, not sure whether to be hurt or annoyed.

"No, of course not, but you do not look like a future princess and that is what you would like to affect, I assume?"

"How did you know?" Grace whispered.

"I have known you loved my son since the first time I saw you two together."

"But *now,* how did you know I wanted to make him see me as potential marriage material?"

"It was inevitable."

"How so?"

"Did you ever wonder why I did not argue against my husband's contracting with King Fahd for the princess to marry Amir?"

"Actually, no. She's a princess, a much more suitable wife to Amir."

"Poppycock…that is what the English say, is it not?" Adara asked in her lilting voice. "We are not living in the Middle Ages, even if the men in my family behave in such a way from time to time."

"If you feel that way, why *didn't* you argue against the arranged marriage?" Grace asked, perplexed.

"Something had to be done to wake up my son."

"But what if he had ended up married to Princess Lina?" Grace almost wailed, remembering all the pain she'd experienced when she thought Amir was going to marry the other woman.

Adara dismissed the possibility with a wave of her hand. "I had a dossier compiled on her. Did you know she is an American citizen?"

"No," Grace breathed in shock.

"Neither did her family, but it was something I discovered. A woman who takes pains to protect her independence is not going to submit to a marriage of convenience."

"But she's a princess."

"She was not raised in her home country. Her father made the mistake of believing bloodlines could insure loyalty when love was what was needed."

"But what if you had been wrong?"

The queen's eyes flashed with arrogant certainty. "I was not." Then she smiled. "I was also right about something else."

"What?"

"You finally realized that with a little

effort you could make my son see that you are what he needs."

"If you believe that, why didn't you say anything before? You knew of my feelings…I know you did."

"Of course. I am not blind, even if my children tend to be."

"So?"

"So…you had to find the strength in yourself to believe in the possibilities. I could not give that to you. Just as Khalil had to find the conviction to fight for his happiness with Jade."

"But…"

"Amir will not be easily caught. You are aware of this. You must not give up. You must have confidence you *can* be the one for him. No other, not even myself, could give you this confidence."

"Except Amir," Grace admitted.

"He has said something? I am surprised. I did not think he was yet open to his true feelings."

"I don't know about any emotions he might have, or not—" and she tended to think *not* "—but he wants me."

"And learning this was enough to give you the courage to embrace your inner beauty?"

"To go looking for it anyway."

The queen waved her hand. "However you choose to see it. I have been eager for this day and am almost as giddy as a girl, now that it is here." She stood up. "Come, we have a great deal to do and our time—as always— is limited."

Grace felt sorry for the young assistant who was told something urgent had come up as she was left to drink the pot of coffee and organize the multiple calendars on her own.

But she didn't have long to pity the other woman as she found herself being driven to the palace airstrip. "Where are we going?"

"Athens. Jade will join us. As will the image consultant I have brought in for just this purpose. She has been staying in the capital city and will meet us at the airport."

"But you couldn't know I was going to come to you."

"I had my plans." And something about the way the queen said it made Grace glad she'd come to Adara on her own.

The trip to Greece went quickly, with the image consultant asking Grace what felt like a thousand questions, but she was sure were probably only about nine hundred and ninety-nine. When they landed at the airport she and

Amir had been at the day before, this time only one person was waiting for them in the courtesy lounge. Well, three if her body-guards were counted.

Jade stepped forward and hugged both Adara and Grace warmly. "So, today is the big makeover?"

"Not a makeover so much as a makeup…we want to bring out Grace's natural beauty and style without losing the things about her that make her so special," the image consultant said.

Queen Adara nodded approvingly. "We are not looking to make a sex kitten out of her after all, even if my son might appreciate that more than anything else."

Jade laughed at this statement while Grace blushed a deep red.

The image consultant, an elegant French woman with skin the color of espresso and height that rivaled Grace's own five foot nine, merely smiled.

"Come, it is time to begin." The queen clapped her hands and, miraculously, body-guards and women were all in motion, headed toward the most exclusive shopping district in Athens.

Sabrina, the image consultant, insisted

Grace have her hair styled and makeup lessons first because the clothing they chose would be influenced by the outcome. Grace usually got her hair cut at shops that allowed walk-ins and she rarely wore the long, kinky red curls down around her face.

"We will start with a relaxer," the master stylist said. "The first time could take as long as three hours. However, when you go in to have your roots done every six months, it will be less time-consuming."

"Relaxer? Every six months?" Grace asked faintly.

The queen did not allow any time to be spent idle, however. She and Sabrina spent the first thirty minutes discussing Grace's color palette. Jade disappeared to have a late lunch with her husband and the queen had food brought in for everyone in the shop.

Exactly three hours later, Grace stared at her image in the mirror. Not only had her hair been "relaxed," but it had been cut as well. Not shorter…but given shape and definition. She was shown how to straighten it into silky waves with a flatiron.

"But you can wear it curly with a little product and still have a lovely style," the master stylist said. "It won't kink now, but fall in softer waves and frame your face nicely."

It had been left long enough she could still pull it up in a ponytail and, for some reason, she was absurdly grateful for that.

The makeup lesson was no less of a culture shock for Grace. The cosmetologist taught her how to apply different shades and combinations appropriate for casual and formal wear, both day and night.

"We'll have another lesson tomorrow, so don't worry if you don't take it all in on the first go," she said.

Grace looked to the queen. "Tomorrow?"

"You cannot expect a change like the one we are affecting to take a mere few hours."

"But Amir—"

"Will survive nicely with his father and eldest brother to keep him occupied."

"Are they in on this, too?" Grace asked, horrified at the thought.

"Of course not."

Her sigh of relief was the last real breath she drew for the next six hours. The group of women shopped more stores than Grace had ever been in if she counted all her previous shopping trips combined. She had never known trying on clothes could be so exhausting. Or liberating.

She'd discovered she liked a lot of the current styles and pretty much detested most of what she had in her wardrobe at home. So why had she worn the clothes? Because they let her hide, but her days of blending into the background were over.

But by the time they returned to Khalil and Jade's home that night, Grace was so tired, she could barely keep her eyes open.

"You've done very well today," the queen said.

"Yes," Sabrina agreed. "You are one of the easiest projects I have had in a long while."

"You call this easy?" Grace asked in a stunned croak.

Sabrina laughed. "It is tiring, yes, but you are naturally lovely and your image needed only to be let out, not created."

Grace wasn't sure she believed the other woman, but she was way too exhausted to argue about it.

Two days later, she stood in front of a mirror in Khalil and Jade's foyer while she waited for the driver to bring the car to return her to the airport. She did not recognize the woman staring back at her and yet she knew her intimately. That was what Sabrina had been talking about.

That woman *was* Grace Brown. The clothing she wore wasn't anything she ever would have bought herself without help, but it also wasn't anything she ever would have turned her nose up at.

The amber-colored, sleeveless button-up blouse had been left open enough to show a hint of her less-than-impressive cleavage, though the outfit highlighted the lines of her body in such a way she didn't look quite so lacking. The lighter shade doe-suede skirt hit her just above her knees, making her legs look really long. And the two-inch heels only enhanced that effect, which Sabrina insisted was a good thing.

Grace could remember the years of being teased as a beanpole, years she'd done everything she could to hide her skinny limbs and disguise her height. Sabrina said her body was trim—not skinny—and actually quite beautiful. Then, to back up her claim, she'd pulled out magazine after magazine that showed women with the same figure as Grace on their covers.

At first Grace's mind had shied away from

the comparison, but even she could not deny the blatant resemblance in body shapes.

The outfit she had on was one they'd seen in one of those magazines and Grace loved it. It was both comfortable and elegant. She felt good wearing it, but also very natural. Not at all like she was trying to be someone she wasn't.

She now had an entire wardrobe's worth of new clothes that covered everything from casual to fancy. All of them fit both her body and her personality…the one that had emerged since she started working for Amir.

The one Sabrina told her she had been hiding with her baggy, nondescript clothes and atrocious haircut. Grace had laughed at the last bit. She'd never known her hair could be so flexible, but she'd worn it in a different style each day, sometimes two—one for day wear and one for evening—and the stylist had made sure she knew how to recreate each one.

She felt confident of the woman staring back at her, comfortable in her own skin and excited to find out Amir's reaction to the change.

She'd realized sometime yesterday what his mom had been talking about in her office though. Grace had had to make this transformation for herself. Not on someone else's urging, or even simply because she was hoping to prove herself on par with Amir.

But because it was time to stop hiding the real Grace Brown.

And that was, in the end, exactly what she had done. Stopped hiding for her own sake. She hoped the new Grace would catch Amir's matrimonial interest, but even if she didn't, she wasn't going back to the woman too uncomfortable with her own femininity to even wear tinted lip gloss.

Heck, now she even knew how to use lip liner, lip color and a shine coat for evenings out.

She smiled and turned toward the door just as Queen Adara arrived in the hall.

She gave the older woman a fierce, impulsive hug. "Thank you."

"You did it for yourself."

"You made it possible."

The queen's eyes were suspiciously moist. "What can I say? I am a woman who likes to meddle in the affairs of others."

Grace laughed out loud.

CHAPTER TEN

SHE WASN'T LAUGHING when she arrived in Zorha, however.

Amir was waiting for her at the landing strip, right at the bottom of the exit step. Dressed in full traditional desert garb, right down to the colored band and *guttrah* that denoted his royalty, he looked as intimidating as she had ever seen him. She'd always felt the desert robes lent an aura of mystery to a man she knew almost as well as she knew herself.

When he donned them, she could all too easily imagine him a sheikh of a bygone era. The one some of his more *interesting* ideas came from.

Regardless of the bright desert sunlight shining down on them now, his countenance was so dark, she wanted to shine a flashlight on him. He was obviously and completely, totally, one-hundred-percent *ticked off*. The look he gave her cohort in crime, his own mother, could have set fire to an ice flow.

The queen merely lifted her cheek for a kiss, which he gave, despite the fact that his muscular, six-foot-four-inch body vibrated with anger. Adara then stepped around him and headed across the tarmac to a limousine, leaving Grace to what she had wrought.

Feeling just a wee bit craven, Grace went to follow the queen, but Amir stepped in front of the bottom stair so she could not hope to pass him. "Where the hell have you been?"

"I left a message for you telling you I would be busy with your mother."

"An e-mail message you knew I would not get immediately," he growled, making it obvious he had not appreciated her form of communication. "You gave no details. You did not answer your phone or respond to my messages. I had to ask my father where Mother had gone in order to discover *you* had returned to Greece."

And that had not sat well with him. He did not like having to go to a third party to learn Grace's whereabouts. She understood, but this time it had been necessary. Had she spoken to him, they would have argued again…she'd still been angry with him the whole time she was in Greece. Though that anger had not diminished her desire to follow through on her plan.

"It was a necessary trip."

"So you say. If it was so necessary, why did you not take me with you?"

"It wasn't related to work."

"So, we are back to the *personal thing,* are we? How is it that my mother is worthy of your confidences and I am not?" he asked, sounding every inch the outraged desert sheikh.

She stared at him, disconcerted that the reason was not obvious to him. "I didn't think you would be up for marathon shopping and makeover sessions. You don't even like shopping for your girlfriends. You make me do it."

And, seriously, how could she trust her own taste, considering the way she used to dress and the stores she frequented? Not such a good idea.

"Marathon shopping? You were shopping for three days?" he asked in a dangerously low voice. "While I wondered if you would be coming back to me, you were out buying, what…?"

"You really can't see?" she asked with disbelief.

His eyes scanned her body and then narrowed, giving her no clue what he thought of the changes. "Makeovers…clothing that is not inexpensive office wear…what is the meaning of this?"

"The meaning?" she asked faintly as the limo carrying his mother and her bodyguards pulled away, leaving her alone with a madman.

Well, sort of alone. The plane staff was still aboard, but not here…on the tarmac with the ultrafurious sheikh who was asking really odd questions.

"Is this for Jerry?" Amir indicated her new look with a wave of his hand. "Do you hope to entice him into being more than your employer?"

"For the last time, I am not going to work for Jerry," she yelled right in Amir's face.

He didn't even flinch. "Then why this?" he asked with another regal wave toward her.

"I did it for *myself.* Can you understand that?"

"I can. Of course I can, but why now, why when we have these unresolved issues between us?"

He considered her impossible-to-miscon-strue letter of resignation an *unresolved issue?* "I needed a break. You needed a break."

"I needed no break. I needed *you*." Then his jaw clamped shut like he wanted to bite the words back.

"I missed you, too," she said softly.

A lot of her anger at him had already resolved itself, but his admission that he needed *her*—not just anyone—helped dispel most of the rest.

"There was no need to do so. I could have gone with you."

"You had meetings."

"And you think they were a pleasure without you? I could not find anything."

She grinned. "You really are helpless without me."

"Do not sound so smug. It is unbecoming."

"My lips are sealed on the subject."

"Do not think I am done being angry with you."

"How long do you think it will last? Perhaps I should ask the pilot to take me back to Greece for a while."

"You will not leave me again." He was all too serious.

"I won't be returning to the palace, either, if you don't let me off these steps."

"I have need of staying very close to you— you might disappear again." Now, why did that sound so suggestive?

"Do what you think you need to." Oh, wow? Was that her flirting? She thought so. And nicely, too. Go her.

"Be assured, I will." The promise in his voice sent messages traveling along her nerve endings. He put his arm out toward her. "Come."

She put her hand on his forearm, feeling his body heat through the sheikh's clothing. "Is this a bad time to mention your mother disappeared along with the limousine?"

"I have my own car."

She looked beyond him and saw the classic Jaguar. "I love riding in it. Thank you for bringing it."

"My motivation was not your pleasure, but I am glad it makes you happy."

"Are you sure? Not even a little?"

He sighed, looking at her with a mixture of perplexity and humor. "Very well, perhaps a bit."

"What was your bigger motivation in bringing the car?"

"I wanted a place to argue without interference."

She laughed. "And now?"

"You are here. I find my urge to beat my chest and make a lot of noise has diminished."

"You really do see me as somehow belonging to you." Couldn't he see how revealing that was of his subconscious thoughts toward her?

"I have said so."

"But Amir, I am your PA, not your girlfriend."

"Thank goodness for that. My girlfriends do not last very long in my life, but your place is much more permanent."

"Have you forgotten my letter of resignation?"

"I am doing my best to, yes."

She didn't know what to say. If this plan to show him she was the right candidate for his marriage plans did not work, she would still have to leave. But she didn't want her imminent departure hanging over their heads, making him angry and her jumpy. She supposed she could deal with it when the time came if she ended up having to leave.

In the end, it was the only viable choice. "We can table the motion for right now."

"It has been tabled." And she could tell that he meant it had been dismissed in his mind before she ever left for Greece.

"Arrogant."

"You are friends with my mother…you know my father…my brothers…you blame me?"

"Just because something is a family trait doesn't mean you have to wallow in it so completely."

"I do not think of myself as arrogant." He opened the passenger door to his car.

She looked up at him, cocking her head to one side as she stepped into the space beside the entrance to the car. "Really?"

"I prefer the term *confident*."

"I'm sure you do."

"You are getting saucy, Gracey."

"Is that a bad thing?"

"Only if you do not want me to do this."

"Wh—" But her word was cut off by his lips.

Hot. Soft. Yummy. Everything she remembered from the night before she'd left for Greece and so much more. She moaned, her body straining toward his as their mouths caressed one another. He felt and tasted *so* good.

His hands skimmed down her torso, leaving zinging nerve endings in their wake. "I like this," he said against her lips.

"Wh-what?"

"The new clothes. They feel good against my hands, but not as good as you are going to feel naked."

"They're comfortable," she mumbled as she renewed the kiss, before the full import of his words sunk in.

Then she went still.

He lifted his head just slightly, his mouth only a centimeter from hers. "Perhaps though, you should go back to your old clothing."

"Why is that?" she asked, but her mind was still grappling with the whole naked thing.

"Because other men will become a nuisance now that your sexy figure is high-lighted by the things you wear."

"You mean like Jerry?" she dared to tease.

"Damn his eyes…he noticed you before the change."

"So did you."

"Remember that, Gracey."

She wasn't sure what he was trying to tell her, but warmth suffused both her body and her heart and she let herself melt against him as her body was so eager to do.

He went back to kissing her, reminding her of the things he had taught her that night in his office and then showing her more. The sound of the stairs being rolled away from the plane followed by a subdued voice infiltrated Grace's mind.

Amir broke his mouth away, his expression pained. "This is not the place."

Grace looked around dazedly. The tarmac was now empty, but the plane was closed and the stairs had been removed. The crew had to have seen them. Would news of the kiss get out?

The royal family were particularly intolerant of gossip, but it could still happen. She couldn't believe Amir had taken such a risk. She stared up at him with a question in her eyes as he gently guided her into her seat because she couldn't seem to make herself move.

He went around the car and got in the driver's side. As the engine purred to life, so did the AC. Grace put her face in front of one of the vents.

Amir chuckled. "Need cooling off, do you?"

"Yes." She was beyond dissembling.

Unrequited love was hard enough to cope with, but fully requited lust was something else all together. Even with the air blowing into her face, she found it hard to breathe. She wanted him to pull the car to the side of the road and make love to her.

"I've never been parking."

"Parking?"

"Making out in a parked car."

"I see where your mind is at."

She looked over at him and his lap. "I see where your mind is at, too."

He laughed, the sexy sound filling the car. "So, finally you look, my little innocent."

She was back to letting the air-conditioning cool her cheeks and she didn't deign to answer. She didn't need her blush to get any hotter.

His fingers carded through her hair. "I like this."

"Less kinky you mean?"

"Oh, I'll like you kinky just fine, Grace, but I like your hair down. It's beautiful."

"You want me to be kinky?" she asked in shock. She *should* have read that chapter on bondage in the sex book.

"I want you to be who and what you are," he said with a smile in his voice.

"But you like my new hairstyle?" she asked. Now that the subject had finally arisen in a normal conversation, she wanted chapter and verse on his reaction.

"Yes. And the makeup. And the clothes," he said, giving it to her and proving once again he *knew* her and cared enough to give what she wanted and/or needed. "Though I liked you just fine before. If you could not tell."

"You never asked me to improve my image to reflect better on you," she said, just now coming to awareness of the truth of that statement.

"I have always found you pleasing, but this look—it seems like the you that has been hiding."

"That's how I felt. I think I spent a long time afraid to try to be anything special in case I failed."

"Because you saw yourself as always less than your siblings in talents and special abilities."

"Yes, but how did you know? I never told you that."

"We have spent a lot of time together in five

years, Grace. I know more about you than probably anyone else."

"Ditto."

"Yes, though my brother comes a close second I think."

"Zahir or Khalil?"

"Zahir, he is very discerning."

"And here I thought he was too busy being the heir apparent to notice others so closely."

"It is part of the job, to be aware. He realized long ago you were a romantic."

"Are you serious?"

"Oh, yes. It embarrassed me to be so slow on the uptake regarding that hidden trait."

"Probably because it was hidden."

"Not to him." Amir sounded unhappy about that.

Grace reached out and touched his arm. "Sometimes, it takes distance to see things. We are very close."

"Yes…and you are very special. All together unique. Do not ever forget this."

"Thank you. I'm a good PA. I know that…it does take special skills to keep your life running smoothly."

"Yes, but you are more than your job, Grace."

"You would never know it by the hours I keep."

"Are you implying I am a difficult boss?"

"More like a straight-out, all-around, high-maintenance person."

"You believe I am high maintenance?" He sounded genuinely surprised.

She had to hide her smile. "I know you are. Don't forget, I know every aspect of your life."

"Except one and soon you will know it as well."

Wow, he was being blatant. "You mean sex."

"Lovemaking…yes."

He was awfully sure of her. "I need to know something."

"What?"

"Am I simply a convenient body?"

"There is nothing convenient about you, Grace. Just as you say I am high maintenance, you are a challenge…a significant challenge to me on many levels. Taking you to my bed will not be easy to keep from my family, nor will it be a simple matter once we are back in New York."

"But it is worth the work to you to make it possible?"

"While you were gone on your unexpected jaunt, I realized I have no choice. I want you, Grace, and I will have you."

It wasn't just confidence…it was desperation born of need. He had to have her and she knew exactly how that felt.

"I want you, too, Amir."

"That is good to know."

"You said you already did."

"That is true, but I find that hearing it is something I needed." His hand covered hers on his thigh.

The intimacy of the action warmed her clear through. "Okay."

"You understand…this thing…this… this…"

"Lust?"

"I am not sure I like that term. *Lust* is a word that can be easily misconstrued. What I feel for you is physical, yes, but you are also my best friend."

That was what she was counting on. "And?"

"And my desire for you…your desire for me…it cannot be labeled as mere lust."

"But it isn't love." She meant for him. She already knew she loved him, but no way did he return the feelings.

"Is that a problem for you?" he asked instead of answering.

"I…" Was it? She wasn't sure, but if she did not take a risk, she would never know if she could have the deepest desire of her heart. "No."

"You have a romantic nature, Grace…you want your first time to be with someone you love."

"I do love you." The words were out and she could not believe she'd said them—nor could she take them back.

"I know…as a friend…I am your best friend and perhaps that is enough for your romantic nature to be appeased," he said as if trying to work it out in his own mind.

She couldn't believe the save. She nodded, too incoherent with relief that he'd misunderstood her compulsive confession to speak.

"I am glad."

He said nothing else and it was only as the silence stretched between them that she realized he was not taking her back to the palace. It was just as she made this realization that he stopped in front of a nondescript building that seemed to be out in the middle of nowhere.

"What are we doing here?" she asked.

"Changing our mode of transportation."

He parked the Jaguar in a garage on the side of the building. Then he led her around to the back and she saw a sand-colored Hummer waiting for them. A man in full desert gear like Amir's, only without the signs of royalty, stowed her bags in the back along with two black leather duffels already there.

"If we were going to change cars, why didn't you bring the Hummer to the airport?"

"I was not sure we would make this trip today."

"Oh…because you were so angry with me."

"And I was not sure why you had left the palace and stayed away. After the things you accused me of, the cruel words I stupidly spoke, I was uncertain how angry you were with me."

It was the first sign of insecurity her sheikh had ever shown her and she was really touched by it.

"I was pretty upset, but I realize you said some of that stuff out of fury at the situation."

"This is most true."

"And I now realize you do want *me,* not just for convenience. That's very important to me."

"As it should be. Be certain, it is true."

"Good." She looked at the Hummer. "You probably didn't want your mom to latch on to the fact we were going into the desert, either. Bringing the Jag to the airport was smart. You can be sneaky that way."

"Only with the best possible motives."

Once they were again on the road, she asked, "Where are we going?"

"Always, it's the questions with you, Grace."

She laughed at his long-suffering attitude. "I'm not likely to change."

He gave her a sidelong glance that did some questioning of its own.

"You yourself said this wasn't a change so much as the real me coming out."

"It suits you, but it is a change. This willingness to be noticed, it is new. But it is good. I like it."

"I think I started taking my first steps away from blending into the walls when I took the job as your personal assistant. *You* don't blend at all."

"And since you are so closely connected to me, you cannot, either."

"No. Not even in my capacity as your PA. People notice me as a way to get to you."

"Or around me."

"Sometimes."

"But they quickly learn that only works when we both want it to."

They shared a smile. "Exactly."

"We make a good team, Gracey."

That's what she was hoping, but she knew that right now, the type of team they were each thinking about was quite different. She had to see if she could get him on the same page as herself.

CHAPTER ELEVEN

"So, WHERE ARE WE GOING, *teammate?*"

He shook his head with a small chuckle. "You are also tenacious."

"It's one of my more endearing qualities. Now, answer the question."

"We are going into the desert. As you can see." At that moment, they turned off the main road and began traveling across the sandy, packed soil toward a set of cliffs in the distance.

"Where in the desert?"

"Someplace we can be alone without my family's interference."

"You're taking me to an assignation? Here in Zorha?"

"As far as my family is concerned, we are on a business trip. It works well that you are my assistant. No questions are asked."

"You lied to your father?" she asked in shock, and just a little awe.

"No, of course not. I merely let him draw his own conclusions."

"Which was that we were going on a business trip."

"Yes."

"But you didn't deny it?"

"He did not actually ask me. He told my brother the plan when he learned I had arranged to be away from the palace for three days upon your return."

"Three days?" *Three whole days of just them?*

"Yes."

"But, they'll figure it out."

"Perhaps."

"And that doesn't bother you?"

"If such a thing were to come to pass, would it upset you?" he asked, rather than answering.

"No. I don't think so, but I also think your father would be furious with you."

"Because you are innocent and under my family's protection?"

"As old-fashioned as I find that attitude, yes."

"Perhaps. It is worth the risk to me."

"But we could wait until we return to New York."

"I have no desire to wait."

Neither did she, but nor did she want him forced into marriage to her by his parents in a fit of outrage. "I'm not sure this is a good idea."

The Hummer stopped. Right there, in the middle of sand, scrub and the barren life of the desert. Amir climbed into the backseat through the open area between his and Grace's seats. "Come here."

She stared at him, feeling a bit like a rabbit facing a snake. "I…uh…"

He put his hand out toward her. "Come here, Gracey. Now."

Her body on autopilot despite the swirling thoughts in her brain, she unbuckled her seat belt and did as he commanded. He pulled her into him and then gently flipped her onto her back along the long bench seat. Then he came down on top of her.

She had to concentrate on not hyperventilating. "I've never had a man on top of me like this," she gasped out.

His big hands framed her face. "That is good to know. I want to be your first in every way, Gracey."

"You will be." She'd never even been kissed. "Wh-what are we doing here?"

"You said you have never been parking."

Parking? He wanted to go parking out in the middle of the desert? "But I thought we were talking."

"No, you were saying things I did not want to hear. Things that might lead to *wait*, or *let's not do this at all*. I am helping you to remember why those words should not pass these delectable lips," he said as he brushed his fingertip over her lips, making them tingle and part.

He slipped his finger inside, pressing it against her tongue. "No more talking, Grace, unless it is to say, *yes, right now* and *more*."

She could do nothing but nod with his finger in her mouth.

He smiled, his white teeth flashing in triumph. "Good girl."

She didn't know what made her do it. Whether it was the condescending phrase he used, or simple curiosity about what it would feel like, but she started sucking on his finger.

Amir let out a groan and thrust his pelvis against her, the long, rocklike hardness of his penis registering as an unmistakable presence. She sucked harder and he pressed her legs apart with his knee, causing her skirt to ride up. His lower body settled more firmly against hers and she felt a zing, like an electric current, go from the apex of her thighs through her body.

She bit down on his finger, then opened her mouth to offer a mortified apology, only to try to garble it around the still present appendage.

Amir hissed out a curse, but it didn't sound angry or even pain-filled. He thrust down against her again, harder this time, and her body responded without her telling it to do so. "More, Gracey…let me feel your teeth."

Oh…oh…he had liked it. She sealed her lips around his finger again, this time letting her teeth scrape along his knuckle.

He moaned and increased the speed and pressure of his movements. She was doing some moving of her own, trying to enhance the sensations of pleasure arcing through her most sensitive flesh. She was wearing thigh-high stockings and panties. The silky barrier between his steel-like erection and her pleasure spot might as well have not been there. His clothes, either, for that matter.

It felt so good, so utterly perfect.

His head was thrown back, the muscles in his neck chording in ecstatic tension. But then he tipped forward and pressed his lips to her neck, biting down with gentle teeth on a spot that made her entire body shake with sensation. It was her turn to moan and thrash as he kept moving in a steady rhythm against her. Then he yanked his hand away from her mouth and took possession of her lips with his own, his tongue immediately demanding and gaining entrance.

Pleasure and tension unlike anything she had ever felt before spiraled through her, increasing until she felt ready to explode.

Amir's hand came up to cup her small breast, kneading and rolling the beaded nipple between his thumb and forefinger. He kept doing it while moving his body against hers until she was going crazy with the new feelings coursing through her. She arched up toward him and he pinched her nipple… hard…and the cataclysm occurred, blasting through her body with wave after wave of pleasure.

She screamed into his mouth, the sensation much too big to keep inside and Amir went rigid above her. His mouth against hers, but no longer kissing, his own rough shout muffled by her lips.

Then he kissed her, passionately, possessively and thoroughly, before lifting his head and staring down at her with eyes that had gone almost pure black with desire. "Do we return to the palace, or continue on, Grace? The risks are worth it to me, are they to you as well?"

There was only one way she could answer that question. "Yes."

She only hoped he came to the conclusion she was the woman for him before his family discovered their affair and demanded redress. She didn't want Amir forced into marriage, no matter how much she craved being bound to him for a lifetime.

The trip out to the desert took an hour from their impromptu parking episode. They were almost to the cliffs when she saw the house. It was such a natural part of the landscape, she blinked her eyes to make sure it was really there. It was.

"What is it?" she asked as Amir pulled the Hummer to a stop in front of the building.

"One of my family's royal hunting lodges."

"Is anyone else here?"

"No."

"It's beautiful…like it's a part of the landscape."

"That was the intention. My great-grand-father designed it."

"How old is it?" she asked in surprise.

"It was built early in the last century."

"Wow. What is it like inside?"

"Come with me and find out." Amir grimaced as he stepped from the big vehicle.

"Is something wrong?" she asked.

He gave a low laugh. "It is nothing."

"What is nothing?" She'd definitely seen a grimace. "Are you hurt in some way, a twisted ankle I don't know about or something? If you are just being a tough, macho guy who should never have left the palace, I am going to be very angry with you."

He shook his head and started laughing for real.

"This is not funny, Amir."

"I assure you, it is."

"Explain what is so amusing about it."

"You, my dear innocent one."

"You think my concern for you is humorous?" she asked, hurt in her voice she made no effort to hide.

He came around the Hummer and took her in his arms. She ducked her head against his chest. She wasn't laughing, but she had taken the time to note he was not limping.

"Gracey…" he said in a cajoling voice.

She refused to look at him. "What?"

"I grimaced because I am uncomfortable."

Her head came up quickly then. "I knew it. You are hurt."

"No, kitten. I am not hurt."

"Then what?"

"I have not found my pleasure while wearing clothing ever. As wonderful as it was, the aftermath is less than pleasant."

She stared at him, not understanding.

"You do know about ejaculation, do you not?"

"Of course I do. I'm a virgin, not an idiot." Then she understood and embarrassment washed over her. "Oh."

"Yes, oh. Definitely not hurt."

"And maybe just a little bit funny," she admitted.

"But sweet, too."

She unbent enough to smile. "I'm glad you think so."

He bent his head down until their foreheads touched. "There is so much about you that I find sweet, my Grace."

"Am I yours?"

"You know I believe so."

Yes, she did and if she needed it to be

something entirely different than a sheikh taking possessive interest in his PA, now was not the time to think about that fact.

He kissed her temple. "You are precious, Grace. So very beautiful."

"It's the makeover."

"It's the woman who stands before me. I wanted you five years ago and I want you now."

Happiness rolled through her in waves and she let it show on her face when she raised her lips for a kiss. He looked at her and then groaned before taking her lips with gentle force.

They stood beside the Hummer, kissing for several minutes until Grace grew light-headed from both excitement and lack of air. Amir pulled his mouth from hers and she gasped in several deep breaths.

He chuckled softly. "Breathe through your nose, kitten."

"Why do you call me that?" she asked as she tried to ignore her blush at his instruction.

He looked pointedly down to where her fingers kneaded his chest.

"Oh."

"And you make soft mewling noises when you are enjoying my kisses."

"Mewling noises, like a cat?"

"Yes. It is very sexy."

"And so you call me *kitten?*"

"I have never called another woman that."

Oh, that admission made her smile. "Thank you."

"Thank you, Gracey. Your gift is beyond measure."

"My virginity?" She knew some people saw it that way, because she could only ever give it once, but her inexperienced condition felt more like a frustrating liability to her than a gift.

"That, too, but the gift of yourself is by far the greatest reward. I think it's time to go inside."

"Yes."

Then, he shocked her by swinging her into his arms and carrying her toward the door. His expression was so intent, she stifled any urge she had to protest or even ask a question. For whatever reason, this was a necessary action for him, and as far as she was concerned it was the perfect thing for him to do. She was not his wife…yet…but she felt like a bride and it was a good feeling.

He opened the door without putting her

down and then carried her inside, stopping just beyond the threshold. "What do you think?"

She'd been so busy looking at him, she hadn't even glimpsed the inside of the house.

She forced herself to turn her attention to it now and gasped. "It's beautiful."

Inexplicable tears filled her eyes. The interior of the hunting lodge would have been impressive enough on its own, but obvious pains had been taken to make it romantic and inviting.

If the outside melted into the landscape, the interior would not have looked out of place in an *Arabian Nights* fantasy. The walls were draped with colorful silks, the furniture was of a bygone Middle Eastern era and the interior structure itself was marked with curves, shaped copper grillwork and recessed alcoves.

But the most impressive feature by far was the main living area. It was sunken two feet and in the center of it was a pile of silks and pillows. To one side was a low table with a selection of finger foods and a pitcher of something to drink. To the other side was another low table filled with candles of different heights, all of them obviously new. Behind the sitting/lying area was a huge fireplace, laid with wood and ready to light.

She didn't know how he had managed to get all the things here. She supposed there were benefits to being royal, but right now all she cared about was that he had cared enough to make the effort.

"Thank you," she said in a choked voice.

"I did not intend to make you cry, kitten."

"It's just so much."

"Too much?"

She shook her head vehemently. "Perfect."

He smiled then, just a small tilting of his lips, but she knew he was pleased. "Your first time should be special."

"How can it be anything else with you?"

He said nothing, but the satisfaction burning in his eyes spoke volumes. He carried her to a room beyond the living area. It was obviously a bedroom. He set her down.

His cheeks were tinged with dusky color. "I need to shower and thought you might want a moment to collect yourself."

"I could do with a change of clothes."

He nodded. "You may find some things in that wardrobe." He pointed to a huge antique armoire.

"If you could just get my cases."

"I'm sure you will find something."

She didn't want to press the point when he'd been so nice, but if he thought she was dressing in some castoffs left by him and his male family members after a hunting trip, he was delusional. She would wait until he got in the shower and then go to get her own suitcases.

He turned and went through an open doorway on the other side of the room that she assumed led to the bathroom. As soon as he was no longer in sight, she crossed to the wardrobe to open the doors. She would have a look so she could tell him she thought it was better to get her own things.

But when the doors swung back, revealing the contents of the armoire, she could not make sense of what she was seeing. Far from some man's hunting garb, even of the sheikh variety, there were several silky caftans in colors complementary to her skin tone. Something she knew now that the image consultant had taken the time to do Grace's color analysis.

Grace pulled out an emerald-green garment shot through with gold embroidery. It would bring out the green in her hazel eyes. She'd noticed the phenomenon when Adara had insisted she try a top on of the same color when they were shopping in Greece.

Grace held the caftan up to herself. It was exactly the right length for her. "How?"

"I had very little to do while you were gone on your jaunt with my mother." Amir stood just inside the bathroom door, his outer robes gone.

Right. The man had had several meetings scheduled and if she had not been so angry with him as well as determined to follow through on her plan, she would have felt guilty for leaving him without her assistance. "I don't understand."

"I went to the bazaar."

"Alone?"

"Zahir was with me."

"He knows you bought these for me?"

Amir shrugged.

Grace was stunned. He had no problem with his brother knowing about them. He'd taken a big risk that his parents might find out about this tryst in the desert. He was far too intelligent not to realize on some level what the ramifications of all this could be.

Once again she had to wonder if he had any clue at all what that said about his subconscious state of mind.

"They're beautiful," she said, indicating the silk garments.

"As are you."

"Because of my new look."

"Because of who you are, my Grace."

A lump of tears formed in her throat and she swallowed it down. "Thank you."

"As I said, the gratitude is mine."

"You aren't taking your shower," was all she could think to say.

"I came to ask if you wished to join me."

"I've never showered with anyone before."

"We could take a bath together." He took a deep breath and let it out. "I cannot forget the image of you in the bath with the petals of my favorite desert blooms floating around your luscious nude body."

"You think my body is luscious?" He'd thought it before the makeover?

"Yes."

"Wow." She thought of all the times she had felt inadequate as a woman next to those he had dated.

She had a choice now. She could continue to compare herself unfavorably or accept that she was the woman he was willing to risk his family's wrath for.

"Does this wow mean you will bathe with me?"

"What if you don't find me as exciting close-up?" she asked, trying to take a practical view of the situation.

But his laugh of incredulity said it all. Then he shook his head. "Not going to happen."

Nothing to misinterpret there.

"Um…I guess, if I get to wear the caftan later."

His eyes glowing with a predatory gleam, he stepped forward. "Count on it. I shall take great pleasure in removing it again."

She made an embarrassing *eep* as he once again swung her into his arms up against his hard chest.

He smiled, the look too primitive for words.

"There are times it is hard to believe you aren't one of your ancestors, rather than a twenty-first century man."

"There are times I feel like one of my ancestors." He carried her into the bathroom.

Her gaze skimmed the room. She'd never seen anything so decadent. Not even at the palace.

"This place does not seem like a bathing room for men all sweaty from a hunt."

"My great-grandfather liked his creature comforts. So did his wife."

"But…he took her hunting with him back then?"

"Theirs was an unusual marriage for the time. They were very much in love."

"He didn't have any mistresses?"

"The royal family of Zorha has always practiced monogamy, Grace."

"That's neat."

"I, too, like that particular aspect of our history."

"You never have cheated on your girlfriends."

A strange expression came over his features. "That is not exactly true."

"What?" she asked in disturbed amazement. He couldn't be telling her he was a cheater. She wouldn't believe it. She knew him.

"Every woman I have been with for the past few years has been a substitute for you, my Grace."

"What? You don't mean that…you can't."

"I do."

"But…" She didn't know what to say.

"I only got involved with Tisa because things had gotten so bad in regard to my desires for you that I had a perpetual hard-on in the office and often outside of it."

The earthy statement rocked her world. "You're kidding!"

"I assure you, I am not. It is not a comfortable condition."

"But you never said anything. You said you knew I wanted you…why didn't you ever try something?"

"You mean why did I not seduce you?"

"Um…yeah."

"I did not want to lose you."

Her brows drew together in a perplexed frown. "Why would you have lost me?"

"My liaisons did not last for very long and once we were no longer lovers, I knew you would leave my employ as well."

He was right. She would have. "But why did it have to end?"

CHAPTER TWELVE

HE DIDN'T ANSWER, just shook his head.

"Amir?"

"This talking…it is not what I want to be doing right now."

"You want to take a bath with me."

"Yes."

"And I must be getting heavy."

"It is a weight I would gladly carry for much longer."

"You say the nicest things."

"I mean them."

"That's what makes them so nice."

"Is it nice to tell you I want you naked?"

"I don't know, but it makes me feel all tingly."

"Tingly is good."

"I think so."

He lowered her slowly to the marble floor,

allowing her body to rub against his on the way down. "Let me remove your clothing."

"I've never been undressed by another person…at least that I can remember." In a family the size of hers, self-sufficiency was learned at a very young age.

"There are many things you have never done that we will do together this night, kitten."

She smiled, liking the endearment as much as when he called her Gracey, or this new "my Grace."

He put his fingers on the top button of her sleeveless top. "You permit me?"

"Yes."

He began to unbutton her top, one slow bit at a time. The backs of his hands brushed her skin and chills broke out along the surface of her skin.

"Amir," she gasped out softly.

"Yes, *aziz?*"

Had he called her beloved? But her thoughts skittered to the four winds as his hands spread apart the edges of her top and then cupped her modest breasts. It wasn't just the feel of his hands on a part of her body that had always been private, but the look in his eyes. He was impacted as profoundly by this touch as she was.

"Please, Amir."

"What do you want, kitten? Tell me."

"I don't know."

"I think I do." With that, he pushed her shirt all the way off, then he reached around her and undid her bra. He pulled her straps down her arms and the undergarment from her body.

The sensation of air against her nipples made them harden even more than they already were, her aureoles puckering around them.

"I..."

"What?"

"I don't know."

His laughter was soft and triumphant. "Just enjoy, my Grace."

"Yessss...."

His hands touched her breasts, skin to skin, and she shuddered.

"That's right, kitten. Enjoy my touch. Allow yourself to experience it completely."

"It's so good," she said on a moan.

"We have barely begun."

"I won't survive."

"I assure you...you will."

"I can't."

"You can."

"Prove it." What was she saying?

But he smiled. "Oh, I intend to."

Then, he kissed her. Not a long, drawn-out kiss, more like a promise.

Her lips curved into a smile as he pulled his head back. "You're very good at this."

"You expected anything less?"

"No, my sheikh, I did not."

"I like that."

"What?"

"When you call me your sheikh."

"For now, you are." And hopefully forever.

"Now is what matters, *aziz*."

"Agreed."

His hands skimmed down her bare skin, leaving pleasure in their wake. "You are so perfectly formed."

She couldn't speak, so she didn't even try.

He undid her skirt, letting it fall to the floor, revealing her garter and panties.

He stepped back and just looked, an expression in his eyes unlike anything she'd ever seen. It wasn't just desire, but she didn't know what else it was, either. Something incredibly intense.

"Amir?" She covered her breasts with her arms.

He reached out and tugged her wrists so she was once again bare to his gaze. "Please…allow me to look. You are so beautiful to me."

"I'm average," she felt compelled to say. Honesty was not always a virtue, darn it.

But he only shook his head. "Believe me when I tell you that you are far from average. Perhaps, there was a time I, too, thought you were like many other women, but my body always knew your unique appeal and my brain caught up eventually."

"But Princess Lina is a pocket Venus."

"She is also married to another man and I could not be happier for it to be so. You are elegant, so very sexy, with the legs of a showgirl and a body that heats my blood to boiling." That look came back into his eyes. "You are everything I want, kitten."

If she didn't know better, she'd think he was trying to tell her he loved her. But even so, what he was saying was plenty special. "You really mean that," she whispered in awe.

"I would never lie to you, my Grace."

"No, I don't believe you ever would. You

have always been honest with me…except when you hid that you wanted me."

"It was there for a woman with eyes. Only yours were luckily stuck on the body parts above my waist."

His meaning sunk in and she blushed, then shrugged. "I would have died of mortification if you saw me looking there."

"Take note, you are welcome to look now."

And she did. Oh, my… His loose-fitting trousers were tented in front of him with what had to be a very impressive erection. No wonder she'd been able to feel it through all the layers of cloth between them in the Hummer.

"You wish to see it?" he asked.

She was not up to teasing him. "Yes."

"Then, by all means…you shall see." He peeled off his shirt and then shoved his cotton trousers down his legs, revealing the most perfectly sculpted male body she could ever imagine.

"You like?" he asked, pride in his voice.

"Ver—" She had to clear her throat. "Very much."

"Now, we finish removing your clothes."

"Okay."

He knelt down and lifted one foot to his

knee, then removed her shoe. She had to hold onto his shoulders so she wouldn't topple over. His skin was so hot, so silky beneath her touch.

He reached forward and kissed her tummy, right below her belly button. She made a noise she did not recognize.

He looked up at her and grinned. "That is right, my kitten."

Oh, man. Her sheikh was lethal.

He rolled the thigh-high down her leg, his warm hands caressing her as he did so. Her fingers dug into his shoulders as sensation upon sensation crashed over her. He gently placed that foot on the floor and then lifted the other and gave that leg the same attention.

She was a mass of quivering nerves by the time he reached up to tug her panties down her thighs. When he kissed her right on the silky curls covering her mound she let out a small cry.

He leaned forward and then his tongue was right there. On her most private place, delving between her nether lips to caress her pleasure button. She started making the "kitten" noises he mentioned in a continuous rotation, so the sounds filled the air around them.

His hands held her hips firmly, not

allowing her to move away as the pleasure started to build from peak to peak until she thought she'd fall right off the edge.

She must have been talking out loud because he said. "Fall, *aziz*. I will be here to catch you."

Her untried body convulsed with such intense pleasure that her knees buckled. He caught her before she could crash to the ground and carried her to the bath.

As they stepped into the fizzing, steamy water, she realized the bath was actually an indoor mineral spring. A plethora of flower petals floated along the surface and even with her brain muzzy from satiation, she realized he had to have put them in…just for her. And he called her a romantic.

The bath was an experience in firsts for her. The first time someone had washed her adult body with cherishing care, the first time she had ever bathed another person, man or woman. The first time she had ever touched a penis. And she liked it. He was hard and soft at the same time. It fascinated her.

He used the time in the inlaid mosaic bathing pool to reawaken her desires and make her intimately aware of his own.

"I want to claim you as mine."

The words soaked into her and even if he didn't mean them the way she wanted most, they caused a primal reaction deep inside her. "Yes."

"You will let me join our bodies?"

"I will." It felt like a vow and she realized that for her, it was.

No matter what he felt toward her, she was giving him more than her body in this act. She was giving him her heart, the part of her soul a lover cherished and as much of her lifetime as he was willing to take. It couldn't be any other way. Not for her. She loved him too much. And she wouldn't want it any other way.

He carried her to the bed, laying her on the divan with careful gentleness.

He began making love to her body all over again and by the time he moved between her legs, she was pleading with him to make her his. But instead of entering her with his hardness, he put first one, then two fingers inside her. It felt so intimate, but so *right,* that she didn't even blush.

"Why?" she asked though, not understanding this part. It felt good, but wouldn't he feel better?

"I am preparing your flesh to take mine. I am not small and you are very tight."

"I didn't know you could do this."

"Be glad that I do."

"I thought you didn't date virgins," she gasped out as his scissoring fingers brushed a spot inside that made her whole body pulse with pleasure.

"I do not."

"Then how did you learn?"

"It is something the males in my family are taught, just as we are taught hand-to-hand combat and warfare with the *gumia*."

"Thank goodness for your ancestors," she said as the blunt head of his manhood probed her entrance a few moments later.

It felt big…and just a little scary. But he went slow, oh, so slow. The pain was minimal, but when he hit the barrier of her virginity she knew to break through would *hurt*.

She didn't care. "Do it."

He kissed her while at the same time touching her pleasure spot with his thumb and just as she was ready to explode into a million bitty fragments of ecstasy, he surged forward. The pain was there, but so was the joy. Such incredible pleasure.

He joined their bodies with passionate force, his own shout of pleasure coming seconds after hers, his heavy body falling like a blanket over hers.

"Sorry," he mumbled into her neck.

"For?" she asked, having not a clue what it could be. He'd given her such intense ecstasy.

"I could not withhold my own pleasure any longer."

"You mean it can be better?" she asked, doubting very sincerely that could be the case.

"I guarantee it."

"This time I really won't survive."

But she did. Again and again over the next three days, as he made love to her out in front of the then lit fire, and then later in the bath, and again in the bed, and even once outside in the desert on a bed of silks and pillows like he had made in the living area of the lodge.

By the time their three-day idyll was over, she had learned infinite ways her body could experience pleasure and almost as many that she could use to give him joy. Neither had spoken of the future and while they were making love, talking and laughing…it did not matter. But now they were headed back across the desert and he had said nothing about what would happen when they reached the palace, much less New York.

She found herself worrying the problem in the back of her mind while he spent the hour-plus drive talking about the history of his family. He'd shared much about the history of his people with her over the years, but this was a lot more intimate a recollection of the past. Despite her concerns, she enjoyed every minute of it.

Until he got to the present day. Or close to it. "I met Yasmine when we were both small children. She was daughter to my father's closest advisor and friend. A princess in her own right, though her father's sheikhdom was defunct and he was part of my father's government."

"When did you realize you loved her?"

"I always knew. There was never a time I thought of marriage to anyone but Yasmine. We made it official when I was eighteen. No one in our families was surprised."

"And then she died."

Amir's face reflected an old pain. "Yes. Then she died."

"I'm sorry. You would be a father by now

if she had lived. One day, you will be a good father."

"I have always believed so."

The last few minutes of their drive was finished in silence, both of them lost in their individual thoughts. She didn't know what he was thinking, but she was remembering the realistic dream she'd had when they first arrived in Zorha.

"We return to New York tomorrow," he said as he pulled behind the same building where they had made their car change three days before.

"I won't unpack when we get back to the palace then."

"Always my efficient Grace."

"It's part of my charm," she teased.

"No doubt. You are invaluable in my life."

"Am I?"

"Yes."

But did he mean what she needed him to mean? Did she have the courage to ask?

She hadn't managed it by the time he pulled the Jag into the palace drive. He came around to let her out of the car.

He reached for her hand and she gave it to him. He pulled her from the car. "We need to discuss the list of candidates for my future wife."

She was still reeling from that pronouncement when the king himself came outside. "Amir, you will attend to me now."

"I need a moment to speak to Grace."

"That will wait."

"No—"

"I am not asking merely as your father," the king said in a voice that brooked no argument.

Amir still looked ready to protest.

"Go with him," Grace said.

The last thing she wanted to talk about was that stupid list. How could he even bring it up right now, after the three days they had spent together?

Amir looked at her. "We need to talk, my Grace."

"Later. Go with your father now."

Amir nodded. "Later."

Then he set his shoulders and turned to join the king. They disappeared into the palace, but Grace did not follow them. She was paralyzed by the pivotal ramifications of the past thirty seconds.

It was the first time she'd ever lied to Amir.

A single word that would forever change

their relationship. Because not only did she have no intention of talking about her final project for him at a later time, but she also had no plans to be there to discuss anything at all.

The decision was made in the same shattering moment her heart froze into painful lockdown. The moment when she realized the last three days had meant nothing to him. She should have known. He'd made no promises, but she had hoped.

They had been so close, more affectionate and intimate than ever before. And not merely physically. It had not just been about making love, but they had spent time talking and simply being together. He had shared his desert with her before on trips they had made to Zorha, but this time, he'd shared how he felt about the land that his family ruled.

And yet he still wanted to talk about the list of candidates for a convenient wife.

What was the matter with her, that he didn't see that she would make the best choice? Was it because she wasn't from a noble family? America had its own class structure, but no recognized nobility and her family certainly would not have been included regardless.

No matter what his reasoning for not wanting Grace as his wife, she wasn't going to stick around bleeding from a lacerated heart while he picked someone else.

She forced leaden legs to carry her into the palace and up to her room, where she picked up the phone and ordered the plane readied for immediate departure. There were benefits to being Amir's assistant. No one questioned her orders, assuming they came from the prince.

All she had to do was pack her remaining possessions and order a car to take her to the airstrip. Then she would be out of Amir's life forever.

"I will not tolerate this behavior, my son."

"I have done nothing wrong."

"You took Miss Brown to the hunting lodge. She is your employee, under your protection." His father's expression was set in stone.

Amir found he was not intimidated. His realization that he loved Grace three days ago had freed him in ways he could never have expected. He felt strong enough to do anything, including stand up to both his father and his king. "She's a damn sight more than merely my employee."

"Ah, so you have figured it out," Zahir said from his position on the other side of their father.

He glared at his oldest brother. "You knew."

Zahir actually grinned. "I am only surprised you did not."

"I did not want to see, so I blinded myself to the truth for five years." And he both regretted and was thankful for that fact.

His fear was that if he had realized he loved Grace earlier, he would have pushed her out of his life to protect himself. But he could not help regret the years he had spent with other women when he should have been with her.

"You are no longer blind?" his father asked, sounding partially mollified.

"No. I see clearly now."

The king looked at his oldest son and then sighed with a frown. "You were right."

"You owe me a camel."

Amir burst out laughing. He should probably be offended, but he found their behavior too amusing. The competition between father and son was fierce. "You two bet a camel on whether I would figure out my feelings for Grace?"

"The bet was on whether or not you would figure it out *before* she left you," his brother said, still looking unnaturally—for him—amused as he answered his mobile phone.

"Grace is not going anywhere," Amir growled.

His brother clicked his phone shut. "I beg to differ with you. She's just ordered the plane to be readied."

Amir was headed out the door to the rare sound of his brother's laughter while his father demanded to know when the wedding was to be.

"As soon as Grace agrees to have me," he called back over his shoulder before taking the stairs to the next floor two at a time.

He burst into Grace's room without knocking. She was packing her computer, tears trickling in slow tracks down her cheeks.

"These unscheduled trips without me have to stop," he said.

Her head snapped up, her eyes filled with wounds he wanted to kick his own backside for. He should have said the words at the lodge, but every time he went to do so, they stuck in his throat. It was his final hurdle off the path set by Yasmine's death.

"You are done speaking with your father?" Grace asked in a low voice.

"We came to terms."

"What terms?" she asked, sounding suspicious.

"He wants a date for the wedding. I told him he had to wait until you agreed to be my wife."

"Then he'll be waiting a long, long time." She turned back to her packing.

Even though he deserved her words, they stung. "Gracey, we need to talk about the list you compiled for me."

"So you said."

"And you agreed to discuss it with me later."

"I lied."

"I must insist."

She spun to face him. "Fine, what do you want to know about it?"

"Why is it missing the only candidate that could possibly work?"

Her eyes widened. "It's a comprehensive list."

"And yet it is missing the only name of import."

"What name would that be?" she asked belligerently, swiping at the tears on her cheeks.

"Yours, kitten. Grace Brown."

"You didn't read the list," she accused, but looking both surprised and pleased at that fact.

"Guilty as charged, but how did you know?"

"My name *is* on it. I was going to pass it off as a joke, but it's there."

He smiled at her intelligence. "You are and have always been the perfect assistant."

"I can't marry you, Amir."

"Why not?" he asked, a tight fist squeezing his gut.

"You want a marriage of convenience and I cannot accept that from you."

He couldn't stand it any longer. He stepped forward and pulled her into his arms. "You might be the best personal assistant in the world, Grace, but you are anything but convenient."

"I mean it, Amir."

"Because you are a closet romantic?"

"Because I love you."

"That is a relief. I should not like to love you more than my country, more than father's good will, more than my own life even and have the feelings not returned."

Her eyes widened with every declaration. "You can't love me."

"Kitten, you might know me better than

anyone else, but even you cannot see inside my heart. I assure you, I *do* love you." How easy he found the words to say after all—when they stood as the final barrier between him and happiness. "More than I ever loved Yasmine, which is why I hid the truth so successfully from myself, I think. Losing her put my heart into stasis for years, but if I lost you, it would be destroyed."

"You're only saying these things because your father insists you marry me." But even she didn't sound like she believed herself.

He smiled and kissed the tip of her nose, then her delectable lips and then lifted his head so their eyes met. "I am saying these things because I realized while you were in Greece that I could not live without you. I still tried to convince myself that we could begin a physical relationship without leading to the loss of my heart, but I was being willfully, stupidly blind. I had already lost my heart so long ago, Gracey, I don't remember a time when you were not the center of my world."

"The other women."

"I will spend my life making up for them—they were cover both to you and to myself."

"When did you realize you loved me?"

"I am ashamed to tell you."

"Why?"

"Because it took me so long."

"Was it when we made love?"

He shook his head. "It was when you stood naked in front of me in the bathing room—that first time. You offered yourself so freely to me and I knew you deserved all I could give you. I also knew that the one thing I had tried to protect myself from had happened. I loved you and if I lost you, I would lose myself."

"No."

"*Yes.*"

"But you didn't say anything…not in three days."

"It was hard," he admitted. "But I planned a special dinner for tonight. I was going to speak my feelings and propose."

"Really?"

"Really."

"I want it."

"The special night?"

"And the romantic proposal."

"Then you shall have it." As long as it was within his power, she would have all her heart's desires.

The romantic proposal was an easy one.

This time his mother had been *his* cohort in crime, coordinating participants while he and Grace cemented their unspoken love at the desert hunting lodge. With his instructions, his mother had organized the perfect evening for a proposal, including a decadent dinner he and Grace fed to one another along with kisses. It was almost impossible to keep his desire for her in check, but he managed it only with constant inner reminders of what was to come.

After dinner, he took her to the lower terrace, where his entire family and hers had been assembled.

Grace turned to him, her eyes shining with joyous tears. "What's going on, Amir?"

Instead of answering, he dropped to his knee in front of her and the entire assembly. "Grace."

"Yes?" she responded in a choked voice.

"I have a position to offer you."

"A position?"

"It is permanent, requires twenty-four-seven on-call status and offers no vacation or sick days. In fact, if you accept you will promise to stick with me through sickness and health. The pay is not that great, but the other forms of compensation make up for that…I hope."

She was laughing and crying at the same time. "Is this your idea of a romantic proposal?"

"I love you, kitten. Will you marry me, *my* Grace, and fill my life with a joy only you can bring?"

She nodded, her mouth open, but no sound coming out. Deciding that was good enough to count as a yes for him, he surged to his feet and took her into his arms, kissing her with all the love in his heart.

Everyone around them cheered.

EPILOGUE

THE WEDDING was a huge event, rivaled only by his brother's marriage to Jade. Their mother, in her element, arranged a wedding worthy of a princess, which was exactly what his Grace was to him.

The queen had made a point of inviting Princess Lina and her new husband, and they came. Amir thanked her for standing up to her family and setting them both free of a marriage that would have made them both miserable. She told him she hoped he and Grace would be as happy as she and Hawk were.

Though they looked like a positively besotted couple, Amir was positive he and his bride would be happier…after all, Grace Brown had been the ideal personal assistant, but she would make the perfect wife.

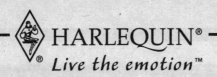

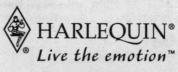

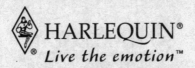

HARLEQUIN®
INTRIGUE®

BREATHTAKING ROMANTIC SUSPENSE

Shared dangers and passions lead to electrifying romance and heart-stopping suspense!

Every month, you'll meet six new heroes who are guaranteed to make your spine tingle and your pulse pound. With them you'll enter into the exciting world of Harlequin Intrigue— where your life is on the line and so is your heart!

THAT'S INTRIGUE—
ROMANTIC SUSPENSE
AT ITS BEST!

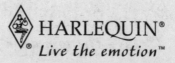

HARLEQUIN®
Live the emotion™

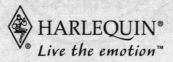

Harlequin® Historical
Historical Romantic Adventure!

Imagine a time of chivalrous knights and unconventional ladies, roguish rakes and impetuous heiresses, rugged cowboys and spirited frontierswomen— these rich and vivid tales will capture your imagination!

Harlequin Historical . . . they're too good to miss!

SPECIAL EDITION™

Emotional, compelling stories that capture the intensity of living, loving and creating a family in today's world.

Modern, passionate reads that are powerful and provocative.

nocturne

Dramatic and sensual tales of paranormal romance.

Romances that are sparked by danger and fueled by passion.

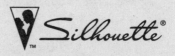